T. H. Safford, De Forest Safford

The Mount Auburn Memorial

T. H. Safford, De Forest Safford

The Mount Auburn Memorial

ISBN/EAN: 9783337288389

Printed in Europe, USA, Canada, Australia, Japan

Cover: Foto ©Andreas Hilbeck / pixelio.de

More available books at **www.hansebooks.com**

Vol. III.   MAY.....1861.   No. 1.

THE

MT. AUBURN MEMORIAL.

A

Record of Rural Cemeteries.

"A Token of all the Heart can keep,
Of holy Love, in its Fountains deep."

BOSTON:
SAFFORD, BROWN, & COMPANY,
No. 15, CORNHILL.
1861.

Terms, $1.50 per Annum, in Advance. Single Copies, 12 cents.

THE

𝕸𝖔𝖚𝖓𝖙 𝕬𝖚𝖇𝖚𝖗𝖓 𝕸𝖊𝖒𝖔𝖗𝖎𝖆𝖑.

New Series.　　　　**MAY, 1861.**　　　　Vol. III.—No. 1.

Hon. JOSEPH T. BUCKINGHAM.

DURING the past month there has been added to our records a name which has always been read with respect, and for many years past with veneration, as the designation of one whose life has been a blessing to the community, and whose departure for the scenes of another world has awakened sorrow in many, very many hearts.

Our own personal acquaintance with the venerable editor, although brief, will ever be remembered as a pleasure. It was something like a year ago that, calling at his request to furnish him with material for a particular article, we held a conversation with him in his library, on various matters which suggested themselves; Mr. Buckingham remarked that his greatest sources of enjoyment were his books and flowers; the latter of which, however, he had just been obliged to relinquish, for he had given up his garden. We grieved for him, that a favorite pursuit should thus be interrupted, and, indeed, it did seem hard that he should long for any gratification so easily attained by the wealthy. The "old man's sorrow for the flowers" we thought deserved the garb of poetry to tenderly express the feelings which influenced him.

He spoke, too, of the pleasure afforded him by a visit to this sacred garden, and here he had another regret to express—his lack of a conveyance over the grounds, for walking fatigued him; he did not speak complainingly of any want, but in a manner which showed how dependent for pleasure he was upon Nature and Art, and how sensibly he felt their influence.

From the newspaper sketches we learn that Joseph Buckingham, son of Nehemiah Tinker, was born in Windham, Connecticut, on the 21st of December, 1779. The father having taken a most active part in the Revolution, employing not his physical exertions alone, but, moreover, throwing in his property for the benefit of the country, the family, at his death, which occurred March 17, 1783, were left destitute of support. Having received some assistance, they removed to Worthington, Mass., in the spring of 1784; and here Joseph was apprenticed to a farmer, and remained in that situation several years, employing his leisure time in acquiring knowledge, thus early showing decided indications of his thirst for information.

His first introduction to the art of printing took place, when he was sixteen years old, in the office of David Carlisle, of Walpole, N. H., the publisher of the *Farmer's Museum*. Not long afterward he commenced work for the proprietors of the *Greenfield Gazette*; he remained at that establishment until 1800, when he changed his residence to Boston. In 1803 we hear of him as prompter in a theatrical company which played in Providence and Salem, during the summer season. In 1806, after applying to the legislature, he changed his name to Buckingham, his mother's family name; this year he commenced the publication of the *Polyanthos*, which existed only for a twelvemonth. In 1809 we find his name attached, as Editor, to the *Ordeal*, a magazine issued weekly. The *New England Galaxy and Masonic Magazine* was commenced in 1817, being published by Mr. Buckingham, with Samuel L. Knapp as his associate in business. Three years after, the Masonic title was dropped, and the publication of the *New England Galaxy* was continued until 1828, at which time Mr. Buckingham disposed of his interest in the magazine. On page 65, Vol. II., a very pleasant article from his pen gives an interesting account of his early struggles in establishing the *Boston Courier*, of which he issued the first number March 2, 1824; which was the commencement of the second daily paper in Boston. Before the end of the fifth week his capital was exhausted, but timely assistance from friends, in conjunction with a fixed determination of the editor to establish such a sheet at all hazards, carried him safely through, and he continued his labors at the *Courier* office until 1848, when he retired from the editorial service. While publishing this paper Mr. Buckingham was not free from other duties, since he continued the *Galaxy* at the same time, and, in 1831, also engaged with his son in the publication of the *New England Magazine* which was issued until 1834, but was then discontinued on account of the death of the younger Buckingham. The *Daily Advertiser* thus continues the sketch:

Mr. Buckingham was several times elected to the Legislature. He was a member of the Senate in 1847, 1848, 1850 and 1851. He was President of the Massachusetts Charitable Mechanic Association for many years. As a conductor of the *Galaxy* he attained an eminent reputation, and no editor in Boston ever wielded a more pungent pen. His talent for satire was unequalled. He was a 'terror to evil doers.' In his feelings he was intensely American, and many foreign adventurers fell under the lash of his keen satire. Kean, the celebrated tragedian, and Mathews, the comedian, he criticised with unsparing severity. But pure, disinterested patriotism he fully appreciated and gratefully acknowledged, although sometimes indulging his prejudices to a degree of bitterness perhaps unnecessary. One of the best editorial articles he ever wrote was published in the *Galaxy*, in September, 1824. It was entitled "National Feeling" being remarks on the visit of La Fayette to Boston at that time. In politics he was an ultra-Federalist, and ever avowed that he should live and die in the faith of the Hartford Convention. In domestic life he was a most affectionate husband and parent. The later years of his life were shadowed by unfortunate investments made in the year 1857.

In the *Saturday Evening Gazette*, of April 26, we find published, in connection with a long article upon his death, a beautiful letter addressed by the venerable editor to his fellow members of the Mechanic Association, under date of March 29, 1858. The occasion of his writing, was a visit which had been a short time before paid him by fifty of his associates in that Society, who met at the Revere House, and proceeded thence to Cambridge, going to Mr. Buckingham's residence in the form of a surprise party.

The letter, as well as giving an account of a touchingly pleasant festivity, will also make the reader acquainted with the social, genial qualities which, by those who knew him best, he was well-known to possess. It was addressed:

"*To Messrs. Uriel Crocker, Osmyn Brewster, John H. Thorndike, and others, members of the Massachusetts Charitable Mechanic Association.*

"My DEAR FRIENDS AND ASSOCIATES—

"The pleasant and unexpected occurrences at my house on Wednesday evening last, demands an acknowledgment, which it was utterly impossible for me to make at the proper time. I need not say to you—for none knew the fact better than yourselves,—that I was taken by surprise. I was not only surprised to find myself suddenly surrounded by a troop of friends, and without a moment's notice—I was amazed, confounded. But when the object of such an unforeseen visit became apparent, these sensations gave way for one of a different character. I cannot tell you how happy I was to mingle in social conversation with so many of my *old* friends and *younger* associates, with whom I had not till then enjoyed the privilege of being personally acquainted. There was the aged, white-haired FAXON, whose feeble and palsied limbs could scarcely support his attenuated frame, his pleasure-beaming eye indicating that there was yet in his heart an apartment large enough to hold remembrances of all his friends; and there, too, was the noble-hearted HARRIS, whose generous purposes and manly virtues, if they had been enshrined in a single individual some three or four thousand years ago, might have averted the fires of Divine vengeance from a devoted city. These, only these two,—were my seniors in age. Would to God I had approached as near to their standard in some of their excellent qualities, as I have in years!

"When you led me to the table you had prepared—affluent in all the ingredients of a sober and rational festivity—I supposed that a few words of recognition, of reminiscence, or of felicitation, were expected from me, but my power of utterance was suddenly suspended. The strong and rapid pulsations of the heart, and a suffocating spasm in the throat, deprived me of the faculty of speech, and compelled me to turn away from the table and the faces of friends to vent, from an overcharged bosom, emotions that I could not suppress. Tears, as pure as ever wet the cheek of man, came to my relief;—but even now, after an interval of four days, I can find no language adequate to the expression of the feelings excited by the occasion; nor can I invent any form of thanksgiving that will not fall far below the grateful emotion with which I receive the parting testimonial of your generous friendship and good-will. There is a certain chord in the heart which, when touched by the finger of sympathy, vibrates with most exquisite melody; but for the description of it no types have yet been fabricated by human ingenuity.

"'To those who feel it not, no words can paint,
And those who feel it, know all words are faint.'

"Friends and brethren, I have been associated with some of you forty-six years,—*forty-six years* of pleasant companionship! As this period of enjoyment is lengthened, the number of those who have partaken of it is constantly diminishing. The earth has not yet firmly settled on the remains of MEANS, WELLS and LEWIS. I am sure that I can offer no petition more available to Almighty God, for the younger members of the Association, than the prayer that they may gather happiness, prosperity, and the consciousness of having well performed the duties of life by emulating the virtues of these honored dead.

"During my connection with the Association, I have been placed in the several offices of Secretary, Trustee, Vice President and President—*all* offices of trust and responsibility,—one of them the highest and most honorable that our Institution recognizes. To have received so many and such repeated testimonials of regard and alliance from an Association like ours, may well justify the honest pride of the recipient; yet I assure you, my friends, that whatever gratification I may have derived from the possession of these posts of distinction, they afforded me not half the soul-felt pleasure that attended the imposition of your kind remembrance manifested on Wednesday, and which I have here attempted to acknowledge. And now, Brethren, before I say *farewell*, allow me to congratulate you on the prospect of returning prosperity in the ordinary labors of life—a prospect which I earnestly hope may not prove deceitful and illusive. I rejoice that you were able to stand firm and erect during the late financial panic, while many an ambitious and bustling operative in trade and commerce was prostrated before the blast. Whatever distinction great wealth and successful speculation may confer on those who covet such supposed superiority, the Mechanics of Boston are the real backbone and muscle on which the body politic safely relies in 'times that try men's souls.' On all such emergencies, their moral and intellectual faculties no less than their physical energies, have been exercised for the general good. Our Association, composed of Mechanics and Artisans, has become an important institution in the social organization of the city. It is not claiming too much to say that no other Association in Boston exerts a more truly beneficent influence, or more justly merits the good-will and regard of the public. Take heed, Brethren, that ye fall not from this high and honorable position, that you forfeit not the good name and enviable reputation you have acquired. 'Let not the gold become dim' nor the fine gold be alloyed by adulteration with any baser metal that may be current in the community. In fine, be true to your motto, 'BE JUST AND FEAR NOT,' and that is the conclusion of the whole matter.

    "Your grateful friend and brother,   JOSEPH T. BUCKINGHAM."

A friend of Mr. Buckingham thus writes in the *Transcript*:

Probably no journalist in New England has drawn his mark so strong, and spread his name so wide, as the gentleman whose burial takes place at Mount Auburn to-day. He has written his last well-turned paragraph and spoken his last bold word; and he continued writing so and uttering himself so, almost to his last day.

I do not propose to enter at all into his private history, or even to touch upon the undertakings of his public career, except to say of each of them, that his character was unsullied, so that, notwithstanding the bitter hostility which his course at different times provoked, no one could impeach the purity of his personal habits or his strict integrity; and for his labors, we may pronounce them extraordinary in their number and variety, their vigor and merit.

But of the man himself a few words. He was made up of strong elements. All his points pronounced themselves keenly. His temper was fervid, and his resolution indomitable. He certainly was not of a meek or quiet spirit. He therefore suffered in the estimation of those who looked at him only from afar and on the outside, and so set him down as a hard, cynical and choleric man. But he was called to trials that would have ruffled a serener nature; and had battles to fight, for which the appropriate accompaniment was not a melody but a cry. And, apart from any consideration of this kind, such unamiable epithets as have been named, would have represented him not only injuriously but mistakenly. They did not really belong to him. He had qualities of thought high up, and of feeling deep down, that were the very reverse of those disturbed and sterner ones, which were so ready to be imputed to him. His mind was eminently contemplative and serious. Great truths impressed it. The finer sentiments kindled and elevated it. He was exceedingly susceptible to all impulses of generosity and gratitude. His heart was a warm one. There was a full spring of affection in him. He was not hopeful. The experiences of his life had not encouraged him to be so; he was not prodigal of courtesies; for he shrunk from few things so much as any suspicion of insincerity or fawning. But he was never so drooping as not to go manfully on; and he was very far from being churlish or rude mannered. They who had only heard of him from a distance, and read the sting of his sarcasm and the vehemence of his invective, never failed to wonder at his mild and unpretending presence. His brow had a strong tendency to contraction. We must admit that. But there were inward dispositions that were smoother than the brow. Every subterfuge of meanness and every show of trickery he hated with perfect hatred; and he was not always so patient as he should have been with the honest convictions that clashed with his own. He was unmeasured, at times, both with the tongue and pen: and did not train himself sufficiently in the endeavor to be otherwise. But the main currents of his will were benevolent; and he knew how to grieve and atone, when he found that his language had been unjust, or that his temper had transported him beyond his better self.

These few words, without commonplaces and without exaggeration—at least so meant to be—are offered to the memory of an old friend. He has lived out all his days. Within a few months, in his sick chamber, he conceived the idea of a new paper, of which he was to be the editor. He even went so far as to write the prospectus, and was scarcely dissuaded from the hardy enterprise. He adhered closely to life. He would not lose,

> "Though full of pain, this intellectual being."

More than at any views that could be presented to him of the future existence, he shuddered at the idea of "falling into nought." This vexed world, now ended for him, was ended mercifully. He literally bowed his head, as if in acquiescence, and slept into death.

MEMORIAL SKETCH OF MISS B———.

THIS young lady, who resided very near Mount Auburn, was first seen by the writer of this article at a small May-day party. Of delicate and refined appearance, she was dressed in white, a soft rose-tint on her fair cheek, and her modest eyes sparkling with pleasure as she held up a bunch of blue violets she had gathered in Mount Auburn. The place had not then been consecrated, and was called Sweet Auburn. She had gathered the blossoms on her way across, an offering to an old lady who had ever been passionately fond of flowers, and at whose house she was visiting. They were received with a pleased and grateful smile, which lighted up the aged countenance with great beauty. The whole scene made a very pleasing impression on the writer.

Some years passed away. Again, in the same parlor, the same parties met. The young lady this time had also brought an offering of flowers, but they were rich exotics of rare beauty and perfume, for it was in March, and the snow lay late and deep. The old lady examined each flower with cheerful interest. They were the last on which her beautiful eyes were ever to rest. For at that moment she was standing on the threshold of eternity, and in a day or two she passed beyond, into the immortal gardens. The vase stood on the table, the sparkling blue waters of the Charles flowed peacefully past, and the golden rays of the setting sun lighted up the countenances of the young girl and her aged friend, so soon to part, and so soon again to meet.

Hardly more than a few weeks had rolled by, when the young girl herself lay down to die. Sweet and patient, the hours of her rapid decline were a holy time to her loving friends. Her mother and sisters rarely left her side, till her lovely spirit hovering on the verge of Mount Auburn, peacefully and silently departed, leaving fond and tender memories to those who knew and loved her.   A. S. O.

E M M A .

TEN years in Heaven!—Ah, yes,
   'Tis just ten years to-day
Since in her life's sweet budding spring,
   Our Emma passed away.

Just sixteen summers had she filled
   A loving daughter's—sister's—place,
Unfolding to our raptured view,
   Each added year, some newer grace.

Oh, it was hard to lay that form
   Of grace and beauty in the dust.—
Yet could I stand beside her grave,
   And with a calm unfaltering trust,

Could raise my tearful eyes to Heaven,
   Pierce through the clouds of grief and gloom,
And see my children in the skies
   Arrayed in full immortal bloom!

And one I saw, who passed before
   Our loved one to the spirit land,
A smile of welcome on his face,
   At Heaven's bright portal, waiting, stand.

Together now they wend their way
   'Mid scenes to mortals all unknown,
Together bow, in transports lost,
   Before the blest Redeemer's throne!

There, ten long years to us; to them—
   Oh, such has been their best employ—
As the first drop on ocean's shore
   To Heaven's full spring-tides boundless joy!

Boston, March 18th, 1861.   E. S. J.

THE MONK OF LA TRAPPE.

BY MRS. NORTON.

There is, among the villages of Saltzbourg, a custom I observed eight years since. When a young priest has received the last orders which enable him to celebrate mass, his relations, his friends, and the whole parish assemble. They choose a beautiful girl, not above twelve years old, whom they crown with flowers. A show of bridal pomp is displayed for the happy couple. They are led to the church, where they are married, and the whole finishes with a gay entertainment; immediately after which, the church recovers her rights.

DURING a spring day of the year 1516, the two young sons of the Count of Altenberg were proceeding on their way, mounted and attended in all the feudal state of those times, from their father's castle, near Zell, in Saltzbourg, to that of their nearest and most friendly neighbor, the Baron Elsenheim. The object of their visit was for the younger brother to take his leave, previous to his departure, on the following day, for one of the great German universities, where he was to complete his education for the church.

The church, indeed, seemed to have "marked him for her own." Augustus of Altenberg was not more than fifteen; yet, even at that early age, the observer was unconsciously impressed with the grave composure of his air, the keen and somewhat haughty glance of his eye, the rare and melancholy smile, which seemed only to soften, not exhilarate, the expression of his countenance. He was tall, his features were regular and very handsome; but his slight figure, and complexion of sallow paleness, indicated the struggle that had taken place during childhood, with the delicacy of his constitution. He had been tenderly reared by his mother, and with her he thought had died the only being who loved him. His father had fixed his affections on his first-born, Claudius, three years older than Augustus, who, buoyant in the full spirits, health and strength of youth, had early shared with his father the toils of the chase, and had lately encountered with him the perils of war. The Count considered his second son as a timid, studious, delicate boy, fit for nothing but a priest.

The brothers arrived at Elsenheim, and were most warmly received by the Baron and Baroness, and by their numerous progeny. After all was said that could be said, about hopes and regrets on the subject of the departure of Augustus, the family crowded round their favorite and far more constant visitor, Claudius; his brother, who seemed more than usually oppressed, withdrew to a windowed recess, and looked in silence on the distant towers of Altenberg, now glancing in the setting sun. The merry laughter of the party grated on his ears and heart. "No one cares about me!" was his bitter thought. At that moment he felt two little hands press his; it was the Elsenheims' youngest child, a girl seven years of age.

"Are you really going away to-morrow, Augustus?"

"Yes, child," he answered pettishly.

"I am very sorry—and for such a long, long time, too—five whole years!"

"Who told you to say that you were sorry, Emmeline?"

The child looked at him, and tears rushed to her eyes. "You do not believe me, then, Augustus? and yet I am very sorry! Who saved my little Pompey, when Edward tied his legs and threw him into the water? Who staid behind with me and helped me along at our last walking-party, when everybody left me, because I could not walk so fast as they did? Who——"

"Well, Emmeline, I believe you are sorry;" and he stooped and kissed the tears from her eyes. "And how long will you recollect me?"

"Until you come back," she said, eagerly. Then, standing on tiptoe, and taking from his vest the gold pin with which it was fastened, "Give me this," she said, coaxingly, "and you will see if I either lose, or give it away, before you come back again!"

And Augustus of Altenberg departed, and the five years passed away.

It was impossible but that the Count, his father, could be otherwise than gratified at the high honors gained by his son at the university; and at the extraordinary reputation which, for one so young, he had established, both for ability and sanctity. It was foretold by all, that he would prove one of the strongest pillars of the church, now trembling to her foundation from the attacks of Luther. He took holy orders, and returned home, where he was received with open arms by his father and brother.

He prepared himself for the celebration of his first mass, by strict seclusion and self-examination; signifying his intention, that, until it had taken place, he would not renew his acquaintance with any of the families round—not even with those with whom he had been most intimate.

The only occasion on which he could not avoid meeting them, was that of the *fictitious marriage;* which, according to the immemorial custom of Saltzbourg, must precede his officiating as a priest. This he regarded as a part of his preparation; as a solemn religious ceremony, by which he would abjure forever those lesser but dearer ties, which bind mankind together, which strengthen our affection to the few and weaken it to the many; for him, no such ties must exist. The arrangements for this peculiar and impressive ceremony were left to his family and clerical friends.

"Emmeline!" exclaimed her sisters, crowding round her, "we have news for you! You are selected as the bride of ceremony for Augustus of Altenberg! We wish you joy!" and they laughed, as poor Emmeline's color came and went at the unexpected intelligence. "You are so fond of him, you know—it will be quite romantic and affecting; be sure you wear the gold pin as conspicuously as possible. Such a bridegroom! I would not marry him, even in jest! I would as soon go over the ceremony with a death's head! But his brother—ay, his brother, is quite a different person. But, come, Emmeline; you look stupified, and our mother is waiting for you."

It was only the day before the ceremony that Augustus was informed of the choice that had been made, of Emmeline of Elsenheim as his bride in form.

Her age, (twelve years), her rank, and the friendship between the families appeared to render the choice unexceptionable. Augustus quite coincided in the opinion. "Emmeline," he repeated musingly—"I remember little Emmeline very well."

" She is springing up into a beautiful girl," observed his brother.

On the following day, the castle of Elsenheim was filled with persons of rank from the surrounding country; and its courts and avenues were crowded with those of the inferior orders, all equally anxious and curious to see this youthful prodigy of learning and holiness.

His appearance, as he descended from his equipage, evidently produced an agreeable surprise; his look and manner of mild affability, free from every thing approaching to pride and moroseness, were by no means what were expected. He was met at the principal entrance by the Baron and his sons, who conducted him, with his father and brother, to the state-apartment, in which a numerous party of gentlemen was assembled.

The easy dignity and calm self-possession of Augustus, contributed to place him at once, in the estimation of the company, in that elevated position which nature and fortune had apparently assigned him. Youth and prudence (a rare union) had overcome all remains of ill-health; his tall figure was no longer languid and bending, but, if not robust, was erect and firm; his movements were strikingly graceful, but manly and decisive; he was still very pale, and no emotion could produce the effect of crimsoning his brow or cheek; on such occasions his paleness, even to his lips, became deadly. His brow was full and lofty; his teeth exquisitely fine; his eye calm, thoughtful and penetrating; it seldom brightened; but when it did, the effect was extraordinary.

He renewed, with apparent satisfaction, his recollection of his former friends, conversing with ease and cheerfulness on the various topics of the day, until his attention and that of the company were attracted by the unfolding of the doors at the upper end of the apartment. The gentlemen immediately ranged themselves along the sides of the room, leaving only the Baron of Elsenheim and Augustus in the centre. The Baroness advanced, leading the bride, surrounded by her sisters, and followed by a numerous train of ladies, all magnificently attired. The two gentlemen stepped forward, and Augustus, kneeling, touched with his lips the hand of this youthful and lovely mockery of a bride; the mother resigned her place, and the little trembling hand remained in that of Augustus.

A strain of solemn music was the signal for the procession to form and move. It was headed by several priests chanting, and youthful choristers waving incense and scattering flowers. The bride and bridegroom went next, followed by their fathers, supporting the baroness; then came the immediate relatives of both families, and the rest of the numerous and splendid company closed the cortege : the halls and passages to the chapel, and the chapel itself, being lined by the retainers of the two noble houses. As they advanced, Augustus looked at his young companion; her eyes were bent to the ground, or every now and then glanced timidly and almost fearfully round. How soft and beautiful were those deep azure eyes, with their long dark fringes! How did the pure blood mantle and recede from the blue-veined temple and the gently-rounded cheek! The little red lips were slightly parted, from excess of awe: the bright, brown, and richly-curling tresses were glittering with jewels, and interwoven with the bridal-rose, while the slight and childish form was scarcely defined through the stiff, embroidered silk, and floating veil which enveloped it.

With a view to encourage her, Augustus pressed her hands and whispered, " Emmeline !" The child returned the pressure, and looked up to him with a smile so full of affectionate gratitude, that it went to the heart of Augustus, and carried with it a sensation unknown before—a sort of doubt, a regret, a still, small voice. (it was the stifled voice of nature,) which whispered at his heart's core—" *Thou* must never be a husband and a father ! "

The gorgeously-lighted chapel, the mitred bishop, the white-robed priests, the living crowds, the solemn music—all that could give grandeur and effect to the ceremony were there. Mass was first celebrated, and then the rite of marriage. The mind of Augustus recovered its tone: there was a sublimity, as a minister of religion, in sacrificing on its sacred altar, the dearest affections of his humanity ! in separating himself forever from his race, in order to become its guide and benefactor !

After the ceremony he slightly touched the cheek of Emmeline. The procession returned to the apartment in the same order in which it had proceeded to the chapel; here Augustus resigned back to the Baroness the hand of her daughter, again mingled with the crowd, and took the earliest opportunity of retiring, leaving the party to enjoy the festivities, in which he had no inclination to share.

He celebrated his first mass, and all Zell and its environs appeared to be present. He preached. The sound judgment, exquisite taste and impassioned eloquence of his discourse took prisoners the hearts of his audience. Nor did those hearts wish to break their bonds; for there was a gentleness, a mercy, a humanly feeling, mixed with his severer admonitions, that dropped balm on the wounds he probed.

A few days afterward, he paid his first visit at the castle of Elsenheim. It was a beautiful evening, and he was informed that the family were about the lake, fishing. Leaving his attendant and horses, he proceeded alone through the well-remembered paths toward the lake. While passing near its head, in a shady and retired spot, he was arrested by a sweet and apparently very young female voice, chanting the evening hymn to the Virgin. He looked, and beheld Emmeline. She was in a child's plain white dress, confined at the waist by a blue ribbon, and her hair fell in natural ringlets over her neck and shoulders. She stood with a small book in her hand, and her eyes were turned upward with a meek and devout expression. He looked at her with much interest for a few minutes, while concluding her hymn, after which he advanced. She sprang toward him, then checked herself, as though she feared her manner was too familiar; but he took her hand and smiled so kindly, that her fears vanished.

" I am glad to see you so well employed, Emmeline."

" I was practising my hymn," she replied artlessly.

" I saw you at church the other day," continued Augustus; " you were far more attentive than any other child of your age."

" Thank you," she smilingly replied, " for saying so; but "——

" But what ? "

" I never was praised for being attentive at church before."

" I am sorry to hear it."

" Ah ! it is very different to hear you preach, Augustus, than to try to listen to poor old Father Anselmo, or to the good fat prior. There was not a word *you* said that fell to the ground ; we all listened, and some of us with tears. When we returned, I wrote down some whole sentences, which I recollected word for word."

Augustus was pleased with the serious enthusiasm of the child, and continued speaking to her for a few minutes, in an advising and paternal strain , they then proceeded to join the rest of the family. As they walked along, Emmeline said to him, " You see that I am not, in every thing, a giddy and thoughtless girl ; " and she drew the gold pin from her sash. " Look ! have I either lost or given away *this* —although it is five whole years since I had it ? "

" What is it ? " inquired Augustus. " I do not recollect it."

Emmeline looked mortified, and returned the pin to her sash, without answering. Their arrival at the fishing-party prevented further conversation.

During the two following years, the time of Augustus was taken up, partly by his clerical duties at Zell, partly in correspondence, both personal and by letter, with many eminent and influential churchmen, on the subject of the heresy of Luther, who now, in spite of all opposition, began to spread his tenets successfully in many parts of Germany. At the commencement of the third year, Augustus was appointed by the Emperor on a mission to the Court of Rome, whither he immediately repaired ; and where, six months after his arrival, he learned the of death of his father.

Some time longer was required to complete the object of his important and delicate mission ; and he was then despatched on one no less so, to Frederick of Saxony, the protector of Luther. In such weighty affairs, none of the confidential servants Charles the Fifth employed, gave him more satisfaction than Augustus of Altenberg, whose moderation, firmness, and quick, clear perception, were rendered the more valuable by his perfect integrity, and his disdain of all the low, cunning arts but too much employed on both sides ; but, above all, by the spotless purity of his life—as the dissolute manners of the Catholic clergy formed one of Luther's strongest weapons of attack.

Augustus was just preparing for his return to Altenberg, when he received a letter, from his brother, the Count, informing him of his approaching marriage, and pressing him to hasten his departure, in order that he might gratify him and their mutual friends, by performing the ceremony. " I do not mention the name of the lady of my choice," continued the Count ; " *that* I reserve to add to the happiness of our meeting, being quite confident not only of your simple approval, but of your heartfelt congratulation."

Augustus arrived at Altenberg, and the brothers met.

"You are about to be married, Claudius," exclaimed Augustus, embracing him. "How devoutly shall I pray that my benediction, on that solemn occasion, may have the power of bringing you all good, and averting all evil! And now, who is your bride?"

"Your young favorite, Emmeline of Elsenheim!"

What a strange compound is the human heart! What feelings, unsuspected by their possessor, lie coiled within its secret folds, ready, at a touch, to start into life! Augustus had, during his journey, frequently amused himself with bringing into mental review all the young ladies of rank in the neighborhood, in order to anticipate the choice of his brother. He was aware that some of the elder daughters of the Elsenheims were married, but two yet remained, older than Emmeline; he thought it very probable that one of these had been fixed on as the Countess of Altenberg. From the idea of Emmeline herself he had always instinctively turned. "She was too young, scarcely sixteen, and was, besides, too serious for his brother; no, *Emmeline* was quite out of the question."

When, therefore, Claudius, with an air of triumph, mentioned her name, Augustus looked and felt surprised. He looked no more, for he was well accustomed to govern the expression of his countenance; but felt with a sudden thrill of pain that the secret sin of his heart was laid open, and that, in its inmost recess, he had cherished a forbidden image. The pang, though acute, was momentary; every power of his vigorous mind rose to subdue and to root out this unsuspected enemy.

"I do, indeed, congratulate you, my dearest brother," he replied, steadily; "if Emmeline fulfill the promise of her childhood and early youth, she is worthy of you!"

"Alas!" sighed the Count, "the doubt is, whether *I* am worthy of her! She is so lovely, so gentle, so pure, so pious, that I can scarcely believe my good fortune, when I think her parents only wait your presence to bestow her upon me."

"Her parents!" repeated Augustus; "but she herself, I trust, gives her affections where they bestow her hand?"

There was a pause. At length the Count replied, "We have often learned from you, brother, that there is no happiness of any kind without alloy; that there is always a drop of bitter, mingled in the sweetest and brightest cup that Providence offers to our lips. Mine is not free from it. Emmeline appears too holy to bestow her affections on any earthly object. She sighs for the cloister, even while preparing, in meek and dutiful submission, to fulfill the wish of her parents. But she is yet so young, that I trust her mind may be easily moulded to another sphere of duty. It shall be the study of my life to make her happy. The natural affections of the wife and the mother will unite with, not supersede, those of the devotee; and she *will* be happy; and I shall be blessed in her being so!" And, as he spoke, the eyes of the Count sparkled with hope; and, recovering from his momentary depression, he continued—"We have decided, Augustus, that you shall have a private interview with her. What you say will have great influence: you will remove her scruples, by proving that a life of active virtue is as acceptable to heaven, as one of devotional seclusion. You will say, I am sure, all that your fraternal affection prompts, and all that your conscience admits."

"Rely upon me, so far," replied Augustus; "but remember, my brother, there is a duty with me paramount to all earthly claims. If I find that she has chosen the better part from deep conviction—if, indeed, the voice of heaven has whispered to her soul, that its pure and spotless sacrifice will be accepted—then, indeed "——

"Then, indeed," interrupted the Count, "the happiness of your brother must not be put in competition with the will of heaven! Be it so! Nevertheless, Augustus, I have such confidence in your enlightened judgment, in your kindly nature, in your freedom from all the sternness of bigotry, that to your hands I commit my cause. You shall decide whether Emmeline shall become the bride of your brother, or the bride of heaven!"

It was now late in the morning; a courier had been despatched to Elsenheim to inform the family of the arrival of Augustus, and the intention of the two brothers to visit them the following day, at noon.

They arrived at the appointed hour, and were received by the Baron and Baroness. After the first welcome was over, the Baron retired with the Count; and Augustus was left, for the moment, alone with the Baroness.

"Your brother has probably informed you, Augustus, that we are desirous you should have a private conversation with Emmeline, and our reason for being so?"

Augustus bowed in acquiescence.

"Then I will send her to you;" and the Baroness left the apartment.

Augustus raised his eyes to heaven, as if to implore both pardon and assistance; then, for a moment, closed them; and folded his hands tightly over his breast, as if, by this external act, to suppress some strong inward emotion.

A light footstep roused him; he looked up and beheld Emmeline. Could two years make such a difference? The bud of promise had, indeed, opened into surpassing loveliness! She was simply arrayed in white; and a transparent veil half mingled with, half shaded her profuse and glossy ringlets. When she entered, she was pale as marble; but, as Augustus approached to meet her, a deep blush gradually stole over her face and neck; she trembled exceedingly, and seemed scarcely able to stand. He led, or rather supported her, to a seat, and, placing himself beside her, struggled to recall the set speech he had made for the occasion.

"I need not say, Emmeline, with what satisfaction I learned, on my arrival, the projected union between our families; how warmly I sympathise in the happiness of my brother, and how grateful I feel to you for conferring it."

He paused. Emmeline made no reply. The vivid, but transient blush had vanished, her eyes were fixed on the ground, and she sat motionless.

"Confirm all this with your own lips, Emmeline; let me hear from yourself, that you freely bestow your heart and hand on my fortunate brother; that you become his wife, and—and my sister."

A deep sigh burst from Emmeline; she looked up to him, her lips moved, but no word found its way. Augustus felt inexpressibly shocked; he knew not what to do, or say. At length a sudden burst of tears relieved the unhappy girl, and for a few minutes she wept in silence.

"Just heaven!" exclaimed Augustus; "can it be thus? Is this marriage, which brings such happiness to us all—is it, indeed, a sacrifice, a painful sacrifice, to you, Emmeline? Speak to me freely; explain to me your motives and feelings, if you think proper to do so; if not, at least, tell me what you wish?"

"The cloister!" she faintly answered.

"The cloister!" he repeated; "but, surely, Emmeline, you are at liberty to reject my brother's suit, from whatever motive, without devoting yourself to the cloister?"

She shook her head.

"You think, then, you do not love him enough to become his wife?"

"There is no one whom I *could* marry that I prefer to him!"

"I am happy to hear that. Your affections, then, are at least disengaged?" She was silent.

"If so, Emmeline, let me advise you. You are very young, and have always been enthusiastically devout; you imagine that the cloister alone leads from temptation here to happiness hereafter; but, let me assure you, that in the fulfilment of the duties of your station, in cherishing the chaste affections of the wife and the mother, you will not be rendered less pure, or less acceptable, in the eyes of Him, whom it is and ought to be your chief desire to please. Moreover, Emmeline, let me warn you, that if, indeed, you meditate the offer of yourself, as a veiled and virgin votaress, at the altar of our holy religion, let me warn you, that such an offering must be without spot or blemish! Search well your heart! Beware that you mistake not the secret workings of pride, of disappointment, of revenge, of any unworthy feeling, or of any unhallowed passion, for the voice of heaven calling you to itself! Beware"——

He suddenly ceased, for Emmeline had fallen on her knees at his feet.

"Mercy!" she exclaimed, wringing her hands; "probe not to the quick a wounded heart! I confess—I am a hypocrite, and as unworthy to be the wife of your brother, as to be the votaress of heaven!"

The astonished Augustus raised her; and, as he supported her in his arms, her head drooped on his shoulder, her light, perfumed tresses veiled his cheek; slowly and timidly she drew his hand to her lips, and her warm tears fell on it, as she murmured, "I have stood at the altar once; there was my faith plighted, my hand given, my love bestowed. Heaven may frown, and earth forbid, but they never can, they never shall be recalled!"

The heart of Augustus throbbed wildly; the best emotions of his nature so mingled with its human infirmity, that the confines of good and evil seemed confounded. The painful struggle was, however, soon over. He replaced her in her seat, and paced the room with steps that every instant became less agitated: at last, he paused before her.

"Emmeline!"

But she dared not look up ; her mind, that, for a moment, had risen with extraordinary power, young and susceptible, was now sinking under the poignant humiliation of having outstepped the boundary prescribed to her sex ; the veil had been withdrawn by her own hand, and she dreaded to meet his gaze.

"Emmeline!" he repeated in a calm, severe tone, "become the wife of my brother, instantly!"

She bowed her head.

"And I, I will to the wars, to take up the cross against the heretics, as my forefathers did against the infidels. God bless you, Emmeline!" he continued in a softened voice ; "let us both strive, by prayer and penitence, to atone for the guilty moment that has passed between us!" And, turning abruptly from her, he left the room.

He returned to her parents and his expecting brother, and thus reported the result of his interview. "Your daughter, madam," he said to the Baroness, "waits but for you to fix the day which shall cement this nearer and dearer union between our two families, so long since united in friendship. May I add my request, that the day be fixed as early as possible ? a wish having been expressed that my counsels, humble as they are, should assist the suffering Catholic nobility against their infuriated and heretical peasantry in Suabia."

Augustus was loaded with thanks, and Emmeline's sisters immediately flew to the apartment in which she had been left.

Fixed in the same seat, with her eyes on the door through which Augustus had disappeared, Emmeline had remained immovable. She heard the approaching footsteps, and started as from a painful dream ; she rose, and, clasping her hands, looked up. "Heaven forgive me if I err ; but *it shall be so!*"

The last words were pronounced with a strong and peculiar emphasis ; they evidently related to the thoughts that had been passing in her mind, and seemed the confirmation of some resolution which, whether right or wrong, she had irrevocably taken. Emmeline advanced to meet her sisters with a serenity of look and manner that surprised them ; they were followed by her parents and the Count ; she gave him her hand, he knelt and kissed it, and, as her affianced husband, saluted her beautiful and blushing cheek. Her eyes glanced hastily round, as though they sought for some one else ; but *he* was gone.

From that moment, the preparations for the marriage proceeded with the utmost rapidity, and the guests were invited for an early day of the following week. Augustus pleaded the pressure of affairs as an excuse for not again making his appearance at Elsenheim, until the day he was to officiate at the ceremony. The demeanor of Emmeline remained calm and placid; she was obedient in all things; often she looked grateful and sometimes pleased. The only peculiarity that was observed, (and it was scarcely observed at the moment,) was her occasionally being absent a considerable time from home alone. In reply to a question from one of her sisters, she begged her not to interfere with or notice her long, solitary, and early walk; that she required an occasional escape from the bustle of the castle, to confer with her own thoughts.

"I generally pay a visit to my old nurse, Wilhelmina, who, you know, is properly a retainer of the Altenbergs, and whose happiness at my approaching marriage with the head of that family, exceeds, I think, even that of any one else."

(To be concluded in June Number.)

REVIEW OF THE FLOWERS.

BY R. F. FULLER.

Now Summer has faded! her favorite flowers,
The gems of the meadow and wild woody bowers,
Where nature's hand planted and cherished, that grew,
And those in the garden, as beautiful, too,
In lovely succession which broidered her train :
No more will we see them, till she come again!
Their high-colored costume, aromatical breath,
Exhaling its sweetness, is scattered in death.
Their beauty was buoyant and faultlessly fair ;
" Immortal " seemed written in loveliness there.
They've faded, except the day-lilies, and those
Where crimson or gold autumn livery glows.
The others in memory live, if at all ;
Their loveliness able again to recall.
—Come, bloom pretty pageant, in verses, once more ;
Which fain would the flowers to blossom restore !

When Spring from the bondage of Winter had burst,
The bloom of the crocuses welcomed her first ;
Through melting March snow-flakes, how sunny they came,
Their yellow flowers lifting like censers of flame !
These bravely the bloom of the Spring pioneer,
Till others take courage and follow them here.
Now cones of blue blossoms the hyacinths show—
Some pink, too, and purple, and white as the snow ;
And then with thick legions of blue melting eyes,
The clustering hosts of the violets rise :
Little skies, *vice versa*, all summer are seen—
" Delights of the ladies," and of angels, I ween !
I call them my darlings—though one of the men.'
The praise of the poets ; who paint with the pen,
With skill, not for picture of beauties like you !
—Nor need any copy the violets blue :
Thank God ! they are faithful with bright balmy cheer,
Each season, and once and again are they here !

When breath of Boreas no longer we dread,
How proudly the tulips are tossing the head!
That gay army, Xerxes once wept to survey,
Shone not in its splendor so proudly as they!
Though women and men may walk in a vain show,
Their outward false glitter, howe'er it may glow,
To rival the tulip is ever denied—
That sceptre and very regalia of pride!

Now forth from the garden our verses extend,
Where May loads of blossoms the apple tree bend;
The cherry branch decking a galaxy bower;
And thick as the sand is the peach's pink flower.
Like drops in the ocean, undistinguished they show;
Each tree is one flower of crimson or snow.
What breath stirs the senses—exciting the blood
To leap through the veins in a merriest mood?
Ah, spring! do not pour all your treasury forth,
In fleeting profusion, to garland the earth!
For it must intoxicate, if in one draught,
These rivers of pleasure by mortals be quaffed;
This quickly-come, quickly-past paradise hour
In pleasure surpasses our compass and power.
Like manna, we cannot preserve it in store
For days which, we see, "cast their shadows before."
Then, Spring! somewhat slower thy beauties bestow;
For riches come quickly, as suddenly go!

The pageant is passing! Like driven snow, see
The fruit blossoms scattered and blown from the tree!
But, here in our garden, the bridal wreath now
Flowers, fit to encircle a garlanded brow.
Each long, flexile twig is all studded with white,
Little asteroid blossoms, as cheerful as light.
The proud dialetra, with flowers arrayed,
As crimson as coral, or lips of a maid,
Grows near in the border a red columbine;
And, climbing the porch, blooms a sweet jessamine.
A white valley-lily its chalice holds up—
How meekly delicious its pure honey-cup!
But, modesty often is neighbor to pride,
And flowers and men often strangely allied;
So, here are seringa—some like its perfume—
And wigelia rosea, a mountain of bloom.
A sweet honeysuckle in series is next;

That cactus beside her we fancy is vexed,
Because its red caverns of gorgeous bloom
Have none of the nutmeg and nectar perfume ;
And this makes us think, as we look at its bloom,
That often the showy want virtue's perfume.

Now see the Scotch roses lead off in their beds
The nation of queens with glory-crowned heads !
A royal sweet unction from each of them flows,
And proves the anointing by God of the rose.
Though never a subject her sceptre obey,
The rose is a sovereign, and sweet is her sway ;
She teaches, in beauty and virtue, that we
Kings and queens by God are entitled to be.
Self-rule is a throne, where each one of us can
Establish the loftiest kingdom of man ;
The spirit's anointing our title shall prove,
Made kings unto God by His heavenly love !

Some roses the hours of sweet Summer outlast,
Perpetual bloom, though the season is past.
They bud, though the rear-guard of asters is all
The train that attends on the steps of the Fall—
Except the day-lilies of milky array,
Their being exhaled in sweetness away !

Farewell, garden flowers ! for soon will be here
A breath, that will turn every blossom to sere !
At last, O ! at last, in a heavenly day,
Shall beauty and bloom never wither away !

THE BRIDE NUN.

"Oh, there lie such depths of woe
In a young blighted spirit: manhood rears
A haughty brow, and age has done with tears—
But youth bows down to misery in amaze
At the dark cloud o'ermantling its bright days."

IT was during the holy week, at the washing of the feet of the pilgrims by the grand-duke of Florence, that I first saw a "*Sposa Monaca.*" The ceremony had drawn together a vast concourse of people, but, thronged as was the immense hall, my attention was instantly arrested by one striking figure. It was that of a girl of about sixteen, perhaps she was older, for the very fair and delicate style of her beauty gave her an appearance of extreme youth, which the lines of the mouth contradicted. The young girl had thought and felt as a woman. She wore a white dress, with white shoes and long gloves—on the head was a chaplet of white roses, and a veil reaching to the feet in graceful folds over the shoulders, which were bare; these and the arms were literally loaded with costly gems. The effect was enhanced by the bonnets and pelisses which made the costume of all the other women present. With that self-satisfied intolerance with which we judge what differs from ourselves, I at first supposed the girl was mad, but seeing no surprise, I inquired and found it was an usage, and they called her the *Sposa Monaca.*

For one month preceding the day fixed to enter the probationary year of noviciate, the *Sposa Monaca* is taken to every public place of resort and amusement, that the world she is to quit forever may appear so alluring, that the sacrifice may be worthy the votary. The dress is such as to designate, at first sight, the destined bride of the church. Elena M—— was she called whom I saw; her history that of thousands past and future. Poor, proud and bigoted, the parents believed that in giving their daughter to the church, they wiped off scores of their own sins, and ensured her happiness in the next world by making her satisfactorily miserable in this.

Elena resisted the purpose of her family with all the energy of a young and passionate nature—burning tears of entreaty and sobbing remonstrances, brought her forced vigils and heavy penance. The struggle had the usual termination; the weaker was the victim, and Elena was led about in triumph, the loveliest and most unwilling *Sposa Monaca* that Florence had known in years. Where for her was the love-dream which makes the life of an Italian? Where the joys, that, like birds of Paradise, flit in the future of maidens? Forbidden all! What had she to do with a cloister, that grave of wrecked hopes and buried memories? She, so young, so beautiful! Yet such is life—

" We do but row, 'tis fate that steers the boat."

How very white she was—a clear, brilliant tint, like that of the snow-drop, as though the hot sun had never shone on her, she looked so fresh and pure—the long dark-blue eyes, and the drooping upper lid, were in keeping with the repose that seemed to have once been the character of her expression—but the pouting scarlet lip of childhood was compressed by the grave thoughts that lip had uttered, and the mouth was stern. I thought of Elena very often that day, and occasionally the next—but on the third day we left Florence to be absent a year, and in the hurry of departure one casts aside torn gloves and worn recollections, as though these were as easily replaced as those, and I thought no more of Elena.

I returned the following spring to the Armida of cities—sweet Florence—and fell into my accustomed ways and means—loitering in galleries, enjoying mornings in studios, with mannakins and their masters, or sitting hours on a stone, like a lizard, just enjoying existence. They told me I had seen everything curious except the taking of the veil, and as I was resolved to have no roe's egg to disturb my peace of mind, I sent to an authority a request for an admission to the next occasion of the kind that might take place.

Shortly afterward I received a line of permission to witness the taking of the veil by Elena M——. Then I remembered her—and I felt almost criminal that she had so long passed from my mind.

The, day came, bright and warm—one of those days in Italian summer where there is a luxuriance of vegetation, a teeming of life, a gushing of light and loveliness that makes the blood flow thick and slow—and you feel

> " Dazzled and drunk with beauty."

And to this fair world Elena was to bid adieu; the thought seemed to fall like a chill shadow on my heart, and I felt one of those mysterious shudders that come to remind us that spirits are about us and around us, and an unearthly presence has moved the " electric chain wherewith we're darkly bound."

Before the altar stood Elena in white, with her jewels as I had seen her the year before—but she herself how changed! There was no trace of youth—years seemed to have condensed their wearing misery into twelve months; the rounded cheek was hollow, and the features were sharp—the lips were white and parted, showing the teeth glittering with unpleasing lustre—life had retreated to the eyes, which glanced like meteors with a restless flickering light. Through the long night she had wept and prayed for release, and hoped until " hope lay mute in its own sullenness "—from troubled, fevered sleep she had started to feel that dull pain of waking which the wretched so well know, when life and daylight return like curses; and when burning sorrow had done its work, searing the heart it scathed, and she sat benumbed and made no outbreaks, because her spirit was broken—then said they, she rejoices to be a nun. Oh! what a tale of crushed passion and dead affection was writ on that young brow!

The service began with pomp and circumstance; as it proceeded they disrobed her, and the long brown hair was cut off—she put on the serge dress and checked veil of the order; the dismal black pall was brought; she shrunk back and looked wildly round. The priest whispered—she appeared not to hear; again he whispered—and then reluctantly and slowly she stretched herself on the marble, and the pall was laid over her. They chanted in low, harsh voices a solemn service; rose-leaves were strewed over the pall—what a sweet mockery!—again they chanted, and so for an hour; then the pall was lifted, and beneath it lay a corpse!

THE hymn commencing, " My country 'tis of thee," usually sung to the tune of America, which has been used so widely for a few weeks past, was composed by Rev. J. F. Smith, of Newton, late Professor in the Theological Seminary of that place. He is also author of the hymns, " The Morning Light is Breaking," and " Yes, my Native Land, I love thee."

LIGHT OUT OF DARKNESS.

I HAD not been blind from my birth. Sitting alone, in the utter darkness, my closed eyes could make pictures. I could call back glories of nature and glories of art, blue sky, and wind-swept fields, and, above all, dear faces, faces whose very memory lightened my night-time—my father, my gentle mother, my young dark-eyed brother. There was another, too, not of our blood, whose face I saw oftener than any. This was strange, for Leona Ashland, the daughter of my mother's most intimate friend, was but a child of ten, six years younger than myself. She was very dear to me, however. She had been in and out of our house as familiarly as a daughter. She was the pet of every one save me; but child as she was, my own feeling for her was too tender and reverent to admit of gay familiarity. I had never heard any one call her beautiful; but to me her face always seemed that of an angel. I used to tremble, lest, some day of summer, God should give her wings, and we should see her no more forever, her features, framed in those long brown curls, seemed so spiritual, so delicate! When I looked into her thoughtful eyes, at school or at church, life seemed a holier, a more earnest thing. But the time came when I could see them no longer.

For fifteen years the world had been visible to me, with its beauty, its mystery, its romance. Then darkness began to steal gradually over me. It was a whole year before the last ray of light had faded. I was stone-blind at sixteen. I was thankful that it was not a sudden stroke. Day after day I had sought in vain for some cherished object of vision. Once it had been the blue range of the far-off hills; again the familiar outline of a distant tree. After a time the darkness came nearer. Day after day some tender grace would fade out from a beloved face, and I could only reproduce it in my fancy. At length I seemed to dwell in a world of shadows. Shapes, whose dim outlines I could only faintly catch, floated by me: but still I could tell day from night; still heaven's blessed light was welcome. But what shall I say of the anguish of desolation when the last ray was gone—when they told me the midday sun was shining clear and bright, and I, alas! sat in blindest, deepest midnight—no light, no hope?

I had so much to give up! It was not alone the joy of sight, the dear faces, the beautiful world; but all my high hopes, my plans for the future, my ambition, my pride. I had meant to be a student. I had had visions of fame. There were months of stormy, surging discontent before I could settle calmly down to my destiny. I secluded myself even from those dearest to me on earth. The very sound of their voices maddened me, for it made more intense the longing to look upon their faces. Day after day I sat in my room, where I had besought them not to come to me.

Sometimes my mother, who loved me more than ever in my sorrow and my helplessness, would steal into the room and sit for an hour beside me in silence. She was so still I could scarcely hear her breathe; but I knew that at these times she wept much. Once, in an irresistible impulse of maternal tenderness, she folded her arms around me and drew my head to her bosom. " Oh, my child!" she cried, " my dear child, be comforted! Believe that there is something left in life, or this blow will kill us both."

But my rebellious spirit would *not* struggle with its despair, even though I felt that it was breaking my mother's heart.

Once—and I think this did me more good than any thing—Leona came to me. She had so long entreated to see me, that at length my mother consented. She came in alone. I knew her footstep as soon as it crossed the threshold; but I did not speak. She came to my side. She laid her hand, her little child's hand, upon mine. I knew, as well as if I had seen it, the sorrowful pity with which her eyes were lifted to my face. She seemed striving to gather self-command enough to speak calmly. At length, low and quiet, yet earnest, her words fell upon my ear: " Oh, Mr. Allen, the rector says God knows just what is best for every one; He is our Father; and He does not love to make us sorry. This is the passage Mr. Green told me to say to you: ' Like as a father pitieth his children, so the Lord pitieth them that fear Him."

Her childish voice had deepened as she recited the words of inspiration. Then she turned to leave me; but I detained her. Already she had comforted me.

" How came Mr. Green to tell you to say that to me?" I asked.

" You are not vexed, Mr. Allen?"

" No; I am grateful. I only wished to know how it happened."

" He was at our house, last night; and he spoke of you. He pitied you very much; but he said you had a great deal left in life yet, if you would not despair. After a while mother went out of the room, and I told him you had been very kind to me, and I wanted to tell you something to make you feel better. Then he said I might repeat that verse to you. Does it do you good?"

" Much good, blessed child! You words have helped me more than you can ever know."

She left me then. I did not strive to keep her. I felt the need of solitude to receive reverently the light, brighter than earthly dawning, which was rising upon my spirit. Her words had thrilled me, as if they had dropped downward from some angel's lips, leaning over the far-off bastions of the celestial city. " A great deal left for me yet in life!" And as I repeated those words my blessings seemed to rise up before me and reproach me. For me, Agur's prayer had been answered. I had neither poverty nor riches; but a competence was mine in my own right, which would secure me against want. I had health and strength, and many friends. The paths about our little village were all familiar to me. I could traverse them without a guide; I could feel the free winds sweep my brow; I could inhale the sweet breath of the flowers; I could hear the beloved voices of home. Verily, God had not forsaken me. I had been wilfully shutting His mercies out of my heart. I knelt now, and thanked Him for what had been left—prayed Him to teach me to bear patiently the loss of what had been taken.

When the bell rang for supper, I rose and went quietly down stairs. They gave no noisy greeting to the son who had not sat beside them there since the spring flowers had blossomed, though now the summer lay green and luxuriant upon hill and woodland. But I understood my father's welcome—the unuttered tenderness which deepened my mother's voice—the eager grasp in which my brother Richard held my hand. I found my plate and my chair in their old place. After that I never secluded myself from them again.

When supper was over I went out to go to evening prayers at the church. I had not thought I could ever go there again. I had dwelt morbidly on the curiosity with which the congregation would look at me. I never thought of that now. God had opened the eyes of my spirit. I went there to thank Him for this great mercy. I had never before been so deeply thrilled with the church music. Hearing seemed to me like a new sense. Through it I drank in deep draughts of pleasure. I had sat in the choir; and when prayers were over I entreated the organist to play for me again. Soon we became fast friends. I think that my enthusiasm pleased him, for twilight after twilight found us alone in the church, with only the little boy who blew the bellows—John Cunningham playing, and I listening and dreaming.

But I soon felt—I think an intuitive sense of power revealed it to me—that the organist was no artist. Sometimes I longed to sweep him off the stool, and interpret with my own fingers the music that was in my soul. This idea that I could be a musician dawned upon me slowly ; but day by day the sense of power strengthened.

At length I asked him to let me try. I think he was astonished. My soul was flooded with harmony. Wild, sweet strains came to me like the whispers of angels. From that night I was the master and he my pupil. Sometimes I would persuade my brother to go with me to the church; and then, for hour after hour, the organ would indeed be the voice of my soul. I breathed out in music all the dreams of my long, dreaming boyhood, before the one stern stroke had come, under which I bowed my head and rose up a man. God was very merciful. With this resource I could never be entirely lonely—wholly desolate.

When I was twenty-one, John Cunningham had left Ryefield, and I had been chosen the organist in our village church. It was my business, for which a small salary was paid me. This was all I was, all I ever could be ; but I was content.

My brother was in college. He was taking my place ; he would realize my early dreams. The world called him a brilliant young man. At home there was little change, save that Leona's light footfall less often crossed our threshold. For some years she had been at school in Boston. In the vacations she came home ; and then I could tell by her voice that she was good and innocent as ever. The next spring—it was winter now—her school-days would be over. At last the time came. Oh, how joyfully I welcomed her, though I scarcely knew why her presence seemed so infinitely precious ! We wandered together into the fields, and she told me how fresh and green the grass was springing under foot—how blue and bright was the May-time sky. I could smell the bloom of the fruit-trees, which were dropping their fragrant blossoms in our path. She never wearied of making all things visible to me. She would tell me how the mist was lying white and purple in the valley—how the far hazy hills were sleeping in the sunshine : and, seeing with her eyes, I scarcely realized that I was blind.

But this dream also had an awakening. My brother Richard came home. He had finished his course at the university with high honors ; and his advent in Ryefield was the signal for a series of parties, and picnics, and merry-makings, in which I could not join, and which took Leona from my side. I heard from all quarters the praises of my handsome, manly brother. He was only nineteen now ; but he was six feet tall, and, they said, looked much older. I was not surprised to hear that his wit and manly graces were making sad havoc with the hearts of the village girls. Already over my soul had began to steal a presentiment of sorrow.

I think my brother loved me very much. He had always made me his confidant. One night he came to my room and said, with a hesitation which seemed very singular in his frank, fearless nature, that he had something to tell me. Then he talked of indifferent subjects for a while; and at length, suddenly— alas, it seemed to me pitilessly !—the blow fell. He loved Leona Ashland ! Oh, Heaven pity me ! God have mercy on me ! I knew in that moment that I too loved her : I—blind, helpless fool that I was !—had made her my idol. I had not known before what was the spell which bound me to her ; or, rather, I had resolutely closed my heart against the conviction. The veil was ruthlessly rent away. I could not choose but look on my own stupid imbecility. A voice in my soul mocked me. It cried : " You—you cowardly idiot !—you thought, did you, to darken her life by fastening yourself upon her ? a blind, helpless shadow ! You thought that young girl could love you—that girl radiant with youth and hope, and all the glory and brightness of life : before whose feet the future stretches out, green, and fresh, and smiling ! You thought you could win her ! Selfish ! insensate ! mad ! "

I bade the voice cease its upbraidings. I shut my ears against it, and desired my brother leave the room. For the first time in my life I was harsh and stern with him. He had a generous temper. I do not think he blamed me. He reproached himself, rather, for speaking to me of a love from which my misfortune had shut me out forever. Begging me to forgive him, he went out.

I shut the door behind him. I locked it. The key turned with a sharp click. Then I threw myself down upon the floor, as a traveller might prostrate himself before the poison-wind of the desert. Lying there, this fierce, scorching simoon swept over me. Unknown to myself I had been cherishing one sweet flower in my heart, watering it, day and night, with the dew of hope. It lay there now, torn up by the roots, its buds blighted, its fair blossom withered.

Blind, helpless idiot ! So the voice in my heart had called me. Ay ; but the blind idiot could *love*. Who else could pour such wealth of tenderness on one who could never grow old to his sightless eyes—whose brow would always be smooth—whose hair would never lose its brightness—whose eyes would never grow dim, because forever he could clothe her with the fair garments of his fancy? And a new voice in my heart answered: "I *am* worthy, for I love."

With those words strength came to me: and I rose up, and stood erect in my darkened world, lonely and grief-stricken, but still a man.

I was not one to inflict my sorrow upon others. I strove to go out into the world with a cheerful face. But I listened with tremulous eagerness to every inflection of Leona's voice when she talked with my brother. I knew she must love him; but there was a curious fascination in watching how this passion would spring up in her pure heart—how the tenderness, which could never be for me, would grow into her beloved voice. Day after day it seemed to me to become full of a sweeter pathos. Richard was constantly by her side. Often they roamed together over the fields. Sometimes they asked me to go with them; but I was too sensitive to intrude. I always refused. Once or twice when I had declined going. Leona insisted on remaining with me. Then she would be so cruelly kind to me, read to me, talk to me, bewilder me with torturing glimpses of an impossible happiness. Then Richard would come back with a floral offering—a spray of honey-suckle, or a bunch of wild roses; and, sitting beside her afterwards, I smelt all day the fragrance of his flowers upon her bosom.

One night she asked me if she might go along with me to evening prayers, as she used before Richard came. It was a pleasant walk, that half-mile between our house and the church, in the summer sunset, with the trees over our heads, all odorous with bloom. There was a curious joy, which was more than half compounded of pain, in knowing that she was by my side, in feeling the light pressure of her hand upon my arm.

When the services were over she asked me to stay a little longer, and play for her, as I had often done before. Hitherto, at such times she had chosen the tunes; but now the fever fit of inspiration was upon me. I poured forth the story of my hopeless love. I used no words, but the music explained itself. It thrilled, it trembled, it pleaded, it despaired, it struggled, it hoped; then, as if for the dead, it wailed, and died out, at last, in a long, helpless cry of sorrow. I heard Leona sobbing. She stood, at a little distance, alone in the darkness. I left my seat. I went to her and took her hands. In the darkness she laid her tender, pitying arms around my neck. I felt her wet cheek against my own. Alas! I knew the language of that silent caress. She loved Richard; but with all the fullness of her angelic nature she pitied me. She would be my sister.

No word was spoken by either of us. We went out of the church, and went home, under the night and the trees.

Soon after this, Richard was obliged to leave us for two or three weeks, on some business for my father. I did not know whether he had declared his love previous to his departure. I watched Leona's voice jealously for signs of sorrow; but it was clear, and full of music as ever. Indeed, I thought it more joyous than was its wont. I said to myself: "How certain she must be of his love, to bear his absence so calmly! The joy of knowing that he is her own forever makes her insensible to sorrow."

Oh, how kind she was to me during those two weeks! It was almost like the old days before Richard came, save that a barbed arrow was rankling in my heart. The unconscious hope I had cherished in those other days could never come back again.

At last the time came for Richard's return. Leona was with us. Frankly, as one who has nothing to conceal, she talked of the pleasure there would be in having him back again. At noon he came. With eager step he entered the room, but his voice trembled when he spoke to Leona. I could only tell by that token how his heart thrilled to be once more by her side. She was not demonstrative. The voice with which she replied to his greeting was very quiet; but I had never known Richard's manner so eager, so restless, as that afternoon.

In the evening we three were alone in the long parlor. I sat at one end among the shadows. Richard and Leona were at the other, where the moon—for I heard them talking of it—shone in at the open window. Perhaps Richard thought I could not hear, or that I slept. He did not know what a second sight hearing is to the blind. Not a murmur, not a quiver of their voices escaped me. It seems that he had never told her of his love before. He poured it forth now with passionate, fervid eloquence. I listened breathlessly for her answer; I held tight to the chair where I was sitting; I commanded every nerve to do its duty; I bade my self-control be vigilant at its post; I would bear the torture without a moan. I waited to hear her low words of love. Her voice fell on my ear. Hush, rebellious heart! thou hast no business to throb so wildly.

" I can not," she says; " oh, I can not! I thought you knew—I thought you must have known—" And here the tender, troubled voice breaks up into pitiful sobs as she beseeches him to leave her—only to leave her. I hear him go out. Then I cross the room; I kneel at her feet; I tell her I have heard all; and then a mad impulse seizes me: I pour out at her feet the libation of my love. I can not help it. Blind, and poor, and helpless as I was, I had dared to love her. I did not mean to tell her. I knew she would never return it. But when I had heard her grieve I had longed so to comfort her; I had wanted her to know how gladly I would die to give her peace.

Oh! how can I tell the story? She did not spurn me. Once more, in the darkness, her tender arms were laid about my neck. For the first time I felt upon my mouth the kisses of her fresh, pure lips. Her words were solemn and earnest: " Do not die for me. Live! live, dear Allen! and, if you love me, let me be your wife."

When our betrothal was made known there was a struggle in my brother's heart. He loved me; he strove to rejoice in my happiness; but he could not stay to witness it. I who knew Leona's worth did not blame him. He left home, the next week, for a year of foreign travel; and, three weeks after, Leona became my wife.

Our wedding was very simple. We chose to be married in the old church, at twilight; for to us that had been the blessed hour of destiny. When the ceremony was over, and the witnesses had departed, we walked slowly homeward under the trees. Leona told me that the moon was flooding all things with a silver rain of peace; and we felt that it would be the emblem of our future.

My wife insisted on a short bridal tour. She must take her blind husband to Boston. I was a little sensitive about exposing my misfortune to strangers. This step seemed unlike Leona; but I wished to please her, and I consented.

The next morning after our arrival we sat alone in our room at the Winthrop House. I wanted to talk to my wife; but she could scarcely listen. She fluttered round the apartment, arranged as I disarranged the furniture a dozen times. I had never known her so restless. Every now and then she would drop down for a moment upon my knee, and, lifting up my face, would cover it with kisses; but even there she would not sit still.

At length there came a tap upon the door, and she sprang hurriedly to open it. There were a few whispered words with the new comers; and then Leona said gravely: "My love, this is Doctor Williams. I have heard much of his skill; and I brought you here because I longed, for my own satisfaction, to have him examine your eyes. I did not wish to mention it at home, for there was no use in making any one else a sharer of my suspense."

Doctor Williams' voice was very kind. I liked that. He proceeded gently with his examination. For five minutes I was in an agony of hope. In fancy I saw again earth and sky, and, dearer still, the sweet face of my bride. Leona held my hand tightly.

At length the doctor's verdict came. I know he pitied us two poor young things, looking to him to crush or confirm a hope as precious as life. His voice trembled. He said, in low, earnest tones: "God soften it to you! There is no hope!"

He went out of the room. Leona closed the door after him, and then came back, and threw herself into my arms. 'I could feel her heart throbbing tumultuously against my side. But she commanded herself, and strove to comfort me. "My poor, poor darling!" she said tenderly, "can you forgive me for disturbing you with this vain trial? I did so long to know the worst! I could not help hoping before. Now, we shall be at rest. It will not be like a doubtful sorrow."

"And you, Leona, can you indeed be content to share a blind man's darkened life?"

She stopped my words with her kisses.

"Hush, beloved! I will be your light, your eyes."

She has kept her word. I miss no pleasant sights or sounds of nature, for in her I have all things. I do not even need to look on her beloved face, for I see it in my heart forever fresh and young and fair. She was but a child when she first aroused me from my blind despair. She was my comforter then; she will be all the days of my life. The two years since our bridal have been full of joy.

A month ago Richard brought home his bride. They call her more beautiful

than Leona : but I do not believe so much soul looks from the eyes they call so
dark and bright. I am full of content. I know, when God's own angels shall
unseal my vision—when, in the everlasting light of Heaven, the blind shall see
again—fairest among women, fairest and truest, will stand by my side, my God-
given—my wife, LEONA !

THE DEAD.

THE dead are the only people who never grow old. Your little brother or
sister that died long ago, remains in death and in remembrance the same
young thing forever. It is fourteen years this evening, since the writer's sister left this world. She was fifteen years then, she is fifteen years old yet. I
have grown older since by fourteen years, but she has never changed as
they advanced ; and if God spares me to fourscore, I never shall think of her
as other than the youthful creature she faded. The other day I listened as
a poor woman told of the death of her first-born child. He was two years
old. She had a small washing-green, across which was stretched a rope that
came in the middle close to the ground. The boy was leaning on the rope,
swinging backwards and forwards, and shouting with delight. The mother
went into her cottage, and lost sight of him for a minute ; and when she returned, the little man was lying across the rope, dead. It had got under his
chin ; he had not sense to push it away, and he was suffocated.

The mother told me, and I believe it truly, that she had never been the
same person since ; but the thing which mainly struck me was, that though
it is eighteen years since then, she thought of her child as an infant of two
years ; it is a little child she looks for to meet her at the gate of the Golden
City. Had her child lived, he would have been twenty years old now ; he
died, and he is two yet ; he will never be more than two. The little rosy face
of that morning, and the little half-articulated voice would have been faintly
remembered by the mother had they gradually died into boyhood and manhood ; but that day stereotyped them ; they remained unchanged.

Have you seen, my reader, the face that had grown old in life, grow young
after death ?—the expression of many years since, lost for so long, come out
startlingly in the features, fixed and cold ? Every one has seen it ; and it is
sometimes strange how rapidly the change takes place. The marks of pain
fade out, and with them the marks of age. I once saw an aged lady die.
She had borne sharp pain for many days with the endurance of a martyr ;
she had to bear sharp pain to the very last. The features were tense and
rigid with suffering ; they remained so while life remained. It was a beautiful sight to see the change that took place in the very instant of dissolution.
The features, sharp for many days with pain, in that instant recovered the old
aspect of quietude which they had borne in health ; the tense, tight look was

gone. You saw the signs of pain go out. You felt that all suffering was over. It was no more, of course, than the working of physical law, but in that case it seemed as if there was a further meaning conveyed. And so it seems to me when the young look comes back on the departed Christian's face. Gone, it seems to say, where the progress of time shall no longer bring age or decay. Gone, where there are beings whose life may be reckoned by centuries, but in whom life is fresh and young, and always will be so. Close the aged eyes! Fold the aged hands in rest! Their owner is no longer old!

LITTLE CHARLIE.

BY MRS. J. H. HANAFORD.

(Suggested by the Death of the little son of Rev. Phineas Stowe, Pastor of the Boston Baptist Bethel.)

SAFE is the child forever,
  Where the little children go,
Who are early called to Jesus
  From the paths of human woe.
Here, toil and pain, and sorrow,
  Each little child await,
But not a tear he sheddeth
  Who enters Heaven's gate.

The children this side Heaven,
  May wander far from God;
But your dear little Charlie
  Is safe, in that abode
Of joy and peace eternal,
  Where the ransomed e'er rejoice,
Where hearts are glad with hearing
  The tender Shepherd's voice.

No sin, no dark temptations
  Your dear one will assail,
Safe in that Heavenly harbor
  He's sheltered from each gale,
And when your mission's ended,
  And you, in peace, shall die,
Your darling boy will give you
  A welcome to the sky.

June, 1860.

CHILDREN AND THEIR CONCERNS.

THE older I grow the more I love children. They are the rose-buds of men and women; their minds folded up have not yet seen the light. The future world is to them a sort of jest and mystery. A theatric spectacle which pleases them with its scenic effects. The very troubles which afterward will weary them enough, when they understand them better, are now hailed as occasions for mirth. Movings, fires, snow storms, any thing that breaks the monotony of life, that calls them from their desk, that affords them an excuse for jumping and shouting, and giving vent to the embryo energies of their natures.

I do not know a more interesting sight in a small way than a crowd of little boys coming out of school with their books and satchels. An irresistible temptation invariably makes me stop and regard the curious faces and droll groups here presented. What a careless, thoughtless, unconscious set of little dogs they are. How totally ignorant and regardless of all that is going on around them. What a complete little ludicrous world of their own they live in. They are scarcely recognizable as belonging to the race of men. They are a different kind of creature, absorbed in different objects, with only miniature hopes and fears. What a line of odd little faces you see in such a crowd! half developed mouths, foreheads and noses.

It is truly interesting to behold the stirrings of these faculties which are to cope with life, to become we cannot conjecture what, which are to lead them we cannot conjecture where, to identify their hereafter, perhaps, with the history of the globe.

The infant whose actions are circumscribed by the walls of the apartment in which he happens to be—of whom mankind knows nothing, who knows nothing of mankind, what may he not become? where may he not set his foot? The little hand now flourishing a rattle may hold the dagger, or a sword, or with the scholar's pen overturn an empire. To think that Luther once wielded only infant toys! You may be looking on a Cicero or a Charlemagne. He may be the founder of a dynasty with the Hapsburgs, the Clovises, the Alfreds, and the Tudors. What visions shall pass before those laughing eyes! What thoughts shall go on beneath that careless forehead! What tainted sentiments may fall from those yet sweet and unsoiled lips! How a few years will change him! What burning passions will grow up in him! That voice, which now with a soft tone utters, "mother," "father," "forgive me," "kiss me." The tender eyes glittering with tears—well may the trembling mother exclaim : " ah, Time ! what wilt thou make of my boy ? "

THERE is a Bible in the library of the University of Gottingen written on five thousand four hundred and seventy-six palm-leaves.

Editor's Table.

The Massachusetts Slain.

WHEN the Chief Magistrate of Massachusetts dispatched his message for the bodies of "our soldiers dead in Baltimore," he could not have dreamed of the magical influence which a few simple words from his pen, would have upon the masses North, East, and West. It is evident that the language was unstudied, perfectly natural, and for that reason the more powerful. Ah! he understands well the human heart who can thus write volumes in a sentence, and his own nature can be destitute of no kindly, sympathetic feeling.

There is not a true woman in the land whose tears have not fallen like rain, while reading that message, and in each heart there has sprung up a regard for our Governor which no future action of his can obscure, and which he can remember as the fruit of the purest thought of his lifetime; even now, when weeks have passed, those words are repeated with a thrill of feeling, and deservedly; they will be handed down to childrens' children, and still be not devoid of power.

What a world of feeling there is in the desire that the bodies of the slain should be *tenderly* cared for; that, bruised and battered as they were while life remained, the temple, out of which but recently a noble spirit had taken flight, should now be sacredly guarded as the body of a MASSACHUSETTS SOLDIER; that no rude throng should press about, with irreverent jest and desecrating handling, (the report of which last we hope was not true), and that the fallen should have the same care and attention they would receive at home.

Such a message has been read with the warmest feelings of gratitude in the hearts of the people at large, who thank God that John A. Andrew holds the high position he does in this Commonwealth; he needs no title hereafter—his name is enough. Can we doubt that this touchingly earnest message, those words flashing along the wires, met with an instant response in the thoughts of the Mayor of Baltimore; if not, that dignitary could be deservedly pronounced devoid of feeling.

There is nothing more solemnly impressive than the grief of a nation, and particularly of a nation of freemen, over the loss of a soldier. What sight has ever been witnessed in Boston more deeply stirring than the uncovered thousands, hushed to perfect silence when the dirge for "our soldiers dead in Baltimore," mournfully, yet gloriously, sounded on the evening air? Ah! then and there, patriotism glowed more strongly; and sweet it seemed to die and thus be honored by all, whose political differences were long ago thrown to the winds, and who respond now to but one watchword—UNION!

Yes, friends, bear our brave Massachusetts soldier tenderly to his last rest; follow the bier with slow and silent steps, for the noble heart but lately enthusiastic in the cause—yours and the country's cause—is suddenly stilled to rest. Gather round him now, and look your last upon one whose name is bright on history's page; gaze, and be grateful that Death can so enwrap an humble mechanic with its own majesty, that many who have passed him by unnoticed in his working garb, are now as anxious for the last look as kindred or friends.

Is not this bond of sympathy which can thus unite rich and poor, high and low, a wonderful tie? Where now is the hauteur and pomp of station or renown? all are equal here in one deep and national feeling.

Lower him gently in his narrow bed; cast down evergreen, and above all, the soldiers' laurel; but leave him now—to hear the clods rattle upon his coffin were too much to bear—let us turn away with only the remembrance that he lies peaceful and quiet below the evidences of our regard.

When the roll of the Massachusetts soldiers is called, and the hastily uttered name meets with no response, mark the quivering lips, not of women or children, but of stalwart men who have battled with the roughest elements of life until it seems strange that tears can dim their eyes; not only tears but sobs from rugged hearts, feelings which it were against nature to attempt to check. The emotion passes; mark now the change from grief to determination: firelocks are held in a grasp of iron, and in each stern countenance we note a look that enemies may well quail before.

Soldiers of '61! who are in the midst of threatening danger, and are exposed in the path of the same destruction which has already diminished your number, yours has been no common feeling for the comrades "dead in Baltimore." Ready to stand firmly to the last in defence of the flag, *our* flag, to that willingness is now added an unalterable resolve that those already fallen shall not be unavenged, and with such potent influence to work upon you, rocks will not be firmer, steel truer, than the Massachusetts soldiery. What hardships and trials and dangers there are before you in the future, time only will reveal; but we are well assured that although you may be destined to lose many, many from your ranks,—which probability may God avert!—none will seem more worthy of remembrance than those whose blood has been the first shed, and that too on the 19th of APRIL, 1861, another link in the chain of history, which may yet be regarded with all the veneration with which we look back upon the glorious 19th of APRIL, 1775.

Random Sketches.

The Davenport Lots.

NUMBERS 1359, 1360 and 1361, of which Charles Davenport, James Davenport, A. Davenport, and Chester B. Grover, are the proprietors, are situated on Spruce Avenue. The appearance of these lots has been much improved by the removal of the iron fence, which has given place to a beautiful granite curbing around the whole. Ample space is given for flower beds on three sides, while the fourth and west side is ornamented with trees of the *arbor-vitæ* species. The corner posts as well as those at the entrance, are elaborately cut and neatly capped with a hemispherical top arising from an octagonal base. Alternating with these are others, of an ornamental nature, which, instead of receiving a second base, rise to a point from the first. This curbing was executed by Hugh Rowe & Co., of old Cambridge.

In the inclosure we find a number of headstones and two monuments, one at the right and the other at the left of the lot. On the north side of the former is perpetuated the memory of "Alven F. Davenport, died in Cincinnati, Ohio, July 14, 1840, aged 8 months. Albert N. Davenport, died in Cincinnati, Ohio, June 6, 1842, aged 9 months; children of Alvah and Nancy F. Davenport." In the rear of the monument we find a headstone to "Nancy D., wife of Stephen Stacy, and daughter of J. and S. Davenport, died in Edenton, North Carolina, October 3, 1849, aged 30." To this is added the epitaph:

> " Dearest Nancy thou hast left us,
> Here thy loss we deeply feel ;
> But 'tis God that hath bereft us,
> He can all our sorrow heal."

A few paces from this are two headstones; one is erected "to Susannah Davenport, died January 17, 1851, aged 73 years." Below this inscription is the significant reminder,

> " Prepare to meet thy God."

The other perpetuates the memory of "Joseph Davenport, died May 28, 1849, aged 76 years." The Scriptural extract is added:

> " Jesus said, I am the resurrection and the life ; he that believeth in me, though he were dead, yet shall he live."

In front of these a substantial headstone, upon which is carved an Egyptian symbol, bears the name of " Lott Davenport, died April 18, 1817, aged 26 years." Below is the tribute:

"Thou art in the grave, my brother,
We have laid thee there with weeping—
The dark-green trees mark the spot
Where thy wasted form is sleeping ;
That form, alone, is all, thank God,
That to the grave is given ;
For we know thy soul, the better part,
Is safe, yes, safe in heaven."

Upon the monument at the right we find inscriptions to the memory of " Sylvia Johnson, died October 25, 1842, aged 63 years, and her grand-child, daughter of Charles and Joan Davenport, died October 20, 1842, aged 3 years and 6 months; Frederick L. Davenport, died September 28, 1849, aged 2 years; Egbert T. Davenport, died August 26, 1851, aged 1 year 11 days; Chester B. Grover, Jr., died February 15, 1849, aged 5 years, 5 months; Frank F. Grover, died September 23, 1852, aged 4 years 7 days; Chester H., died May 6, 1841, aged 4 years; Bennet B., died May 7, 1841, aged 21 months 15 days." In the rear of this, upon little tablets are inscribed the names—" Frank," " Chester," " Bennet," " Charles H.," " Mrs. Johnson," " Georgianna," " Frederick," and " Egbert."

Lot of Benjamin Rich.

This inclosure is on the south side of Indian Ridge, just opposite Forest Pond, an advantageous situation; this contains a tomb, the top of which is neatly turfed; the front is of granite. Upon the turfing stands a plain monument having inscribed upon it the words of the Saviour:

"I am the Resurrection and the life ; he that believeth in me though he were dead yet shall be live ; and whosoever liveth and believeth in me shall never die.—St. John vi: 25, 26."

Below this we find an inscription in memory of Benjamin Rich, born December 12, 1775, died June 3, 1851; Susanna, wife of Benjamin Rich, born August 16, 1773, died August 22, 1848. On the other sides we find the following names: " Susanna, born December 17, 1804, died November 14, 1805; Lucy, born August 11, 1737, died March 4, 1821; Benjamin, born June 9, 1802, died April 12, 1829; Caroline Virginia, born May 14, 1830, died July 15, 1833; Benjamin, born October 26, 1834, died September 30, 1836; Susan Rich Larkin, born April 22, 1842, died November 10, 1847.

Lot of Mary Haines.

No. 1402, on Beech Avenue, near the Chapel, is a pretty little lot, appropriately fenced; it belongs to Mary Haynes. Rosebushes and ornamental trees adorn the inclosure; a grave plot in one portion is covered with myrtle, and above it a headstone is " Sacred to the memory of our dear mother, Sarah Haynes, wife of Edward Haynes, who died January 27, 1837, aged 64 years; removed to Mount Auburn August 29, 1846." It is also " Sacred to the memory of our father, Edward Haynes, who died August 26, 1846, aged 79 years; interred August 29." These lines are added:

" May angels watch this grave,
Till Gabriel's trump shall sound
To wake the slumbering dead ;
The redeemed shall rise to live
With Christ, the living Head."

" This was erected by their daughters."

The Prince Tomb.

The Prince tomb is situated on Geranium Path, in close proximity to the statue of " Father Ballou " on Central Avenue. It is one of two built together, the first bearing the name G. H. Gray, and this simply that of Prince. The location is rendered very pleasant by the numbers of shade and ornamental trees in this vicinity. Directly in front, and belonging to the lot, are two arbor vitæ trees, tall and symmetrical; on the other side of the avenue two goodly sized maples present such an appearance as only maples can in spring; and just seen between the branches, a graceful larch in the background completes a beautiful picture. Many trees near the tomb have not yet unfolded their leaves, so that the effect which is to come is yet in the future of the spring.

Fine advantages for adorning the front are presented in the long flower-beds placed next Geranium Path, from its junction with Central Avenue to the sharp turn on the left, as the path crosses to Beech Avenue.

Here rest the remains of Miss Caroline Willey Cunningham, a native of Columbia, S. C., daughter of Mrs. Albert G. Prince, and grand-daughter of the late Nathan Willey, Esq., of Boston. She died in the village of Hyannis, on the 23d of December, 1858, after having nearly attained her nineteenth year.

The following touching tribute to her memory was published in the "Atlantic Messenger" of December 30, on announcing the event.

"Death hath its mission as life hath. If death were denied to us in this mortal estate, the dwellers on this planet would soon sink into the grossest sensualism. The love which our Heavenly Parent gives for relatives and friends, and which death itself cannot obliterate, is one of the strong proofs—if not the strongest—of God's intention that beyond the dim veil of this life we shall be reunited, in the divine order, with those whose existence has been the light and joy of our own. If we have been sordid and worldly before the death of one who, above all others, we loved the most, such an event has a tendency thence to inspire in us a higher spirituality. If we are so happy as to possess a full conviction that our loved departed is henceforth to be an angel to watch over us through the term of our mortal life, it will make us the more heedful of our conduct lest by word or deed we grieve their pure spirits and mar their heavenly peace.

The subject of this notice was personally little known to the writer; yet from the little he had seen of her, and from the much he has learned of her character from those who knew her best, it is his privilege to say that she was moulded in a form of rare spiritual beauty. Before us lies a book her appreciation of which is attested by its marked passages. It is 'The Poets of America.' Bryant's 'Thanatopsis' is among the marked poems. We judge her to have been serious and pensive above her years. But most of all must we admire her for her Christian graces. These made her unapproachable by those temptations which so frequently lead to ruin the soul that has not Christ formed within it, the hope of glory. Patient was she through all her illness, and gentle and soothing were her words to those near and dear to her. We close with one of the most memorable sentences she gave in charge of the nurse to her brother. 'Tell Charlie, Carrie is in Heaven, and that she will keep watch over him as his guardian angel.' May her pure life and her triumphant death prove a lasting spiritual blessing to her family and friends."

In the succeeding issue of the same periodical we find another sketch, written by "one of her friends."

> "'Another's hand is beckoning us,
>   Another call is given;
> And glows once more with Angel steps
>   The path which reaches Heaven.
> Our young and gentle friend whose smile
>   Made brighter summer hours,
> Amid the frosts of winter time,
>   Has left us, with the flowers.'

Few, but her most intimate friends, knew the rich stores of thought and feeling in Carrie's mind. Reserved to strangers, and apparently cold and distant; but to those she knew and loved, she was confiding and trustful, and lavished on them the most devoted attentions, and often astonished them by the revelations of a soul, pious without bigotry, refined and sensitive, yet strong in good judgment and common sense, that balance wheel so often wanting in such finely organized natures. The voice of duty was to her a talisman, to call forth all the energies of her being.

> 'Her heart ever open to Charity's claim,
> Unmoved from its purpose by censure or blame;
> While vainly alike on her eye and her ear,
> Fell the scorn of the heartless, the jesting and jeer.'

But Carrie has passed on to a more genial sphere, there to unfold and expand in the purer air of that blessed clime, and may her sorrowing friends all feel that " the good die not."

'God calls our loved ones but we lose not wholly
    What he hath given:
They live on earth in thought and deed as truly
    As in His heaven.''

The Tour.

UPPER ELM AVENUE.

We commence our monthly tour upon Upper Elm Avenue, on the west side of the grounds. The first inclosure, on the corner, at the right, near Mistletoe Path, is No. 2004, the lot of Josiah M. Jones. Three lots in succession on this side, of which the one mentioned is first, are fenced with the same pattern of palings but with different posts, which, in this instance, rise some two feet above the bars; the pattern of fence used is neat and appropriate. The situation of the lots here is good, since the slight rise upon which they are located causes them to overlook quite a number on the south side, among which the Magoun monument is situated; while on the other side of the avenue the handsome granite Knight monument is in full view. The monument in No. 2004 is an elaborate little Gothic structure, erected to the memory of " Henry A. Reed, died May 20, 1852, aged 29 years." Below we find inscribed:

" No more to suffer, but for aye to be
In God's eternal sunshine, blest and free."

In No. 1956, of which Solomon Piper is the proprietor, we find a marble monument consisting of plinth, base, die and shaft; on the north side is an inscription " In memory of Jerusha, wife of Solomon Piper, who died August 20, 1851, aged 71 years." On the south side is perpetuated the memory of " Susan Esther, daughter of Solomon and Jerusha Piper, died August 18, 1820, aged 1 year 5 months and 27 days." No. 1897, the inclosure of Susan Sears, contains a marble urn-topped monument. Upon the north side of the die a beautiful wreath is carved, and below it is an inscription to the memory of " George

Sears, born September 8, 1790, died October 12, 1845; Susan Sears, born January 3, 1798, died August 7, 1860." On the west side: " George Sears, Jr., born May 3, 1830, died September 15, 1830." On the east side: " Olive Sears, born June 9, 1822, died April 28, 1832; Susan Gray Sears, born June 12, 1825, died April 26, 1832; Olive Gray Sears, born March 7, 1828, died May 10, 1832." At the left of the monument a marble headstone bears the name of " Lydia Richards, born February 19, 1810, died November 4, 1852." In the rear of the lot are five scroll headstones in memory of " Oliver," " George Sears," " Susan Sears," " Susan," and " Oliver." The first one and last two bear the symbol of a broken bud. The next lot, numbered 1889, is that of Elizabeth Wyeth; it contains a scroll headstone erected to the memory of " Ann Susan," over whose grave myrtle and flowers are planted. No. 1885, of which Josiah Stedman is proprietor, is very neatly fenced and adorned in front with spruce trees and shrubbery, the latter of which, just leaved out, gives a fresh appearance to the front. Above the die of the monument a tall shaft rises; in the south-east corner three little headstones bear the names of " Henry," " Josiah," and " Sophia." Adjoining the Stedman enclosure is No. 1884, the lot of Frederic W. Sargent; the fence is of a plain and suitable pattern; between this and the next lot a fine young maple has just expanded its leaves. Upon the monument, which is of marble and well carved, the common but ever appropriate symbol, a full-blown rose broken from the stem, is employed above the inscription to the memory of " Helen Janvrin, wife of Frederic W. Sargent, and daughter of Dennis Janvrin, died May 14, 1849, aged 21 years."

The Memorial.

We here present our readers with the first number of our monthly *Memorial*, and although we are aware that the present is an unfavorable time for the change which we have made, we still hope that its visits will be as welcome as those of its predecessor.

Record of Interments at Mount Auburn Cemetery.

Numb.	Date (1861).	Name of Deceased.	Where from.	Age. y. m. d.	Date of Death.	No. of Lot.
10,266	March 27	Edwin A. E. Merriam	Roxbury	23 4	March 25, 1861	1293
10,267	28	Elizabeth Whiting	Cambridge	75 2 27	27,	1017
10,268	28	William Borroughs	Germantown,	39 1 24	24,	3053
10,269	30	Thomas Lannon	Boston [Pa.	58	Jan. 16,	456 S. J's
10,270	31	George E. Richardson	Cambridge	23 9	March 26,	R. T.
10,271	31	Helen A. Howard	Roxbury	11 21	29,	1914
10,272	31	Drusilla Doolittle	Boston	46 4	27,	2346
10,273	31	Frederick O. Haskell	Boston	1 9 17	29,	457 S. J's
10,274	April 1	Henry Keyes.	S. Hadley	66 3 14	29,	1740
10,275	4	Charles F. Howe	Boston	36	April 1,	2964
10,276	4	Charles Wyeth	Cambridge	23 11 27	4,	3040
10,277	4	Abiel Wyeth	Cambridge	32	Aug. 3, 1841	3040
10,278	5	Elizabeth McDonald	Boston	57 11 14	April 3, 1861	R. T.
10,279	5	F. E. French	Charlestown	24 11	2,	R. T.
10,280	6	S. Augusta Carleton	Boston	31 6 17	2,	458 S. J's
10,281	6	Daniel A. Greene	Charlestown	18 9 29	4,	459 S. J's
10,282	7	W. D. Austin	Dorchester	36 7	4,	159
10,283	7	Robert L. Tilton	Beverly	1 5	5,	1763
10,284	7	Farnsworth	St. Louis	33	1,	402
10,285	8	Mary E. Stevens	Boston	65 9 18	6,	1146
10,286	8	Child of G. S. Mitchell	Boston		6,	2524
10,287	9	Jane S. Hanaford	Montague	47	7,	1955
10,288	9	Charles C. Smith	Cambridge	33	8,	460 S. J's
10,289	9	Fannie B. Corey	Worcester	23	Jan. 22,	2256
10,290	10	Joan Farrington	Boston	29	April 8,	461 S. J's
10,291	10	Maria A. Mudge	Jamaica Pl'ns	48	7,	351
10,292	10	Charles H. Robinson	Boston	6 1 8	Jan. 28, 1816	2661
10,293	11	James Brown	Malden	4 10 28	April 8, 1861	734
10,294	11	Jessie Louise Brown	Malden	2 7 9	9,	734
10,295	11	Alfred Smith Wright	Boston		10,	2635
10,296	11	Mary Hale	Boston	26 10	9,	1931
10,297	11	Caroline A. Billings	Charlestown	4 5	Dec. 28, 1838	1420
10,298	11	Sarah Billings	Charlestown	68 2	April 9, 1861	1420
10,299	11	William Billings	Charlestown	50	March 25, 1840	1420
10,300	13	Jane R. Greene	Boston	57 8	April 11, 1861	963
10,301	13	Amasa G. Smith	Somerville	52	Nov. 22, 1852	3088
10,302	13	Joseph T. Buckingham	Cambridge	81 3 21	April 11, 1861	149
10,303	14	Amelia C. Schuchmann	Boston	11 4 6	12,	462 S. J's
10,304	15	Nathan Haskell	Chelsea	75 11	12,	R. T.
10,305	17	Harriet G. Duncklee	Brighton	47 1 11	16,	483
10,306	17	Child of N. H. Earle	Boston		16,	1909
10,307	18	Ann H. Fairbanks	E. Abington	50 5	3,	802
10,308	18	Eve Maria Kelley	Boston	84	17,	2024
10,309	18	John Downes Austin	Boston	34	Feb. 28,	159
10,310	20	Nathaniel I. Bowditch	Brookline	56 3	April 16,	1461
10,311	21	Augustus W. Bowen	Boston	23	17,	R. T.
10,312	23	Rebecca Prescott	Boston	64	20,	2856
10,313	24	Joseph E. Mansfield	Boston	21 4	22,	463 S. J's
10,314	25	Maria W. Passaron	Springfield	61	Jan. 25,	212
10,315	25	John Clear	Boston	8 6	April 23,	2060
10,316	25	Maria Brown	Boston	17	23,	R. T.
10,317	26	Son of C. J. Underwood	Boston	5	26,	1082
10,318	26	Child of W. F. Smith	Boston			2774
10,319	26	Henry Evans	Boston	3	23,	155
10,320	27	Elijah Thayer	Boston	70 2 25	25,	2449
10,321	28	Charles E. Bowen	Newton	63 8 10	25,	1940
10,322	29	Catherine Edwards	N. Beverly	66 10 16	27,	707
10,323	29	Frederick T. White	W. Newton	1 1 19	27,	2884
10,324	30	Eloise Hartman	Boston	24 9	28,	773
10,325	30	Ann Maria Sawyer	Charlestown	27 6	28,	3093
10,326	May 1	Louise S. Estabrook	Belmont	40 1	28,	1983
10,327	1	Esther Stone	East Boston	49	28,	461 S. J's
10,328	1	Everett P. Bond	Medford	1 3	Oct. 15, 1858	1991
10,329	2	Thomas B. Park	Boston	28	Sept. 11, 1860	1462
10,330	2	William Saunders	Cambridge	73 11 15	April 29, 1861	1105
10,331	2	Henry C. Jones	Boston	1 1 12	Aug. 7, 1852	3006
10,332	2	Sarah Louise Cumings	Boston	1 11 16	Jan. 20, 1852	694
10,333	2	Caroline M. Cumings	Boston	1 28	Nov. 18, 1844	694
10,334	2	Pelham Bonney	Boston	59 2 8	April 29, 1861	3095

Vol. III.   JUNE.....1861.   No. II.

THE

MT. AUBURN MEMORIAL.

A

Record of Rural Cemeteries.

"A Token of all the Heart can keep,
Of holy Love, in its Fountains deep."

BOSTON:
SAFFORD, BROWN, & COMPANY,
No. 15, CORNHILL.
1861.

Terms, $1.50 per Annum, in Advance. Single Copies, 12 cents.

THE

𝕸𝖔𝖚𝖓𝖙 𝕬𝖚𝖇𝖚𝖗𝖓 𝕸𝖊𝖒𝖔𝖗𝖎𝖆𝖑.

Vol. III.—No. 2. JUNE, 1861. New Series.

JAMES THOMSON.

JAMES THOMSON, the author of "The Seasons," was born at Ednam, a couple of miles or so from Kelso, Scotland, on the 11th of September, 1700. His father was the minister of the parish, and it was intended to bring him up to the same profession. The early childhood only of Thomson was spent here, for his father removed to Southdean, near Jedburgh, having obtained the living of that place.

Of Thomson's sojourn at Southdean, nearly all that is now known is comprehended in the following passage in Mr. Robert Chambers' "Picture of Scotland:"—

"'The father of James Thomson was removed from Ednam to this parish while the poet was a child; and here, accordingly, the author of 'The Seasons' spent the days of his boyhood. In the churchyard may still be seen the humble monument of the father of the poet, though the inscription is nearly obliterated. The manse in which that individual reared his large family, of whom one was destined to become so illustrious, was what would now be described as a small thatched cottage. It is traditionally recollected that the poet was sent to the University of Edinburgh, seated behind his father's man on horseback, but was so reluctant to quit the country for a town life, that he had returned on foot before his conductor, declaring that he could study as well on the braes of Sou'den—so Southdean is generally pronounced—as in Edinburgh."

Here Thomson undoubtedly acquired that deep love for nature, and that intimate acquaintance with it, which enabled him to produce the poem of "The Seasons," which, with considerable faults of style, is one of the richest compositions in the language, in the legitimate subject-matter, in the grandeur of its scenery, drawn from all regions of the earth, and in the broad and beautiful spirit of its religious philosophy.

His father had died two years after his return to Edinburgh, leaving his mother with a considerable family, who raised upon her little estate, by mortgage, what she could, and came to reside in Edinburgh. James resolved not to weigh upon her resources longer than needful, but set out for London with his poem of " Winter " in his pocket. He had introductions to several influential persons, and one of them to Mr. Mallet, then tutor to the sons of the Duke of Montrose. His great want, Dr. Johnson says, on reaching London, was a pair of shoes. To make his calls, these were necessary, and his " Winter " was his sole resource. It was a wintery one, for he could find no purchaser for it for a long time, and when purchased, it did not for a good while sell. At length it fell under the eye of a Mr. Whatley, who instantly perceived its merit, and zealously spread the information. Thomson was quickly a popular author, and from this time resided chiefly in the neighborhood of London.

The Chancellor conferred on him the place of Secretary of the Briefs, which made him independent. On the death of the Chancellor Talbot he lost this post, through being too indolent to make application to Lord Hardwicke for it, though Hardwicke kept it open for some time that he might. For a time he was again reduced by this circumstance to poverty and difficulty. Out of this he was, after a while, permanently raised through the influence of Lord Lyttleton, a pension of a £100 a year being conferred on him. This removed the pressure of utter necessity, but compelled him to work, without which compulsion, perhaps, no man would have worked less. About three years before his death, Lord Lyttleton being then in power, made him Surveyor-General of the Leeward Islands. Those islands he surveyed from his elevation on Richmond Hill, and very general his survey of course must have been. The particular and actual survey was left to his deputy in the islands themselves, and Thomson netted a yearly balance, the deputy being paid, of £300 a year, which, with his pension, left him most comfortably at ease in the castle of indolence. Besides his two principal poems, he wrote several tragedies, as " Sophonisba," in which the unfortunate line,

" O Sophonisba, Sophonisba, O ! "

was parodied by a wag, with

" O Jemmy Thomson, Jemmy Thomson, O ! "

and was echoed through the town everywhere and for a long time. " Agamemnon " was another, " Edward and Eleonora " a third, and " Tancred and Sigismunda " his last and best, except a posthumous one—" Coriolanus."

That no man lived more completely in a castle of indolence there can be little question, and perhaps as little that it cut his life short. He died at forty-eight, of cold taken on the Thames between Kew and Richmond. He used, it seems, to be in the habit of walking from town to his house at Richmond, and crossed at a boat-house somewhere here about, which being also a public house, he there took a rest and refreshment. The place is still shown. Here, it would seem, he came warm from his walk, and, crossing in a damp wind, took cold; but this susceptibility to cold was the direct result of his indolent, self-indulgent, and effeminate habits. Had he followed those practices of healthy activity so finely described in his poem, how much longer and more useful might his life have been! Yet it must be a fact unquestionable, that Thomson, as a boy, rose early, saw both sunrises and all the glories of nature, plunged into the summer flood, and braved the severity of winter. No man could so vividly or so accurately describe what he had not experienced, and they who know best the country know how exact is his knowledge of it. Every one can feel how masterly are his descriptions of the grandest phenomena of nature in every region of the world, when such descriptions are deducible from books. In those, however, which came under his own eye, there is a life, and there are beauties that attest his personal knowledge.

(Concluded from May Number.)

THE MONK OF LA TRAPPE.

BY MRS. NORTON.

WILHELMINA had become a widow and a mother about the time of Emmeline's birth; and, with the permission of the Altenbergs, she became her nurse. It was difficult to say whether the good woman was more fondly attached to her own little son, or to her foster-child. Emmeline certainly possessed unbounded sway over her. Nothing could rouse the feelings, or sharpen the intellects, of the indolent Wilhelmina, who was snugly settled in a cottage on the Elsenheim territory, except what related to these two objects of her care. Her son had accompanied one of the younger Elsenheims on his travels, and she was, at present, devoted heart and soul to Emmeline.

The castle of Altenberg, so long without a mistress, was also in full preparation to receive the young and beautiful bride of its lord; who, himself, all hope and happiness, with perceptions not sufficiently acute and delicate to perceive aught in the meek and evidently reluctant submission of Emmeline, except the natural effect of her timid and maidenly feelings, spent the greater part of his time at Elsenheim, gazing on the treasure a few days were to make his own.

Emmeline's sisters observed that the day previous to that fixed for the marriage, she was pensive and irritable. She had taken her early walk as before; but, about twilight, she managed to slip out again; and, returning in a short time, appeared more pleased and cheerful than they had yet seen her. She changed her dress; and, joining her family, met the Count, who was late in his visit, with more of satisfaction than she had ever testified. The evening passed delightfully; and, on parting, the Count fondly embraced his affianced bride.

The family were summoned to an early breakfast the following day.

"My morning walks are now over," said Emmeline smilingly, to her sisters; "but I shall retire for an hour or two to the oratory; and, whenever I am required to be dressed, you will find me there."

About noon, the magnificent equipage of the Count of Altenberg drove up to the gate, and the brothers alighted. Augustus proceeded straight to the chapel, and, having robed in the vestry, took his station with the other officiating priests. It was the first time he had been in this chapel since, four years past, he himself had enacted the part of bridegroom to the beautiful girl he was now about to bestow on another. The chapel was illuminated and decorated precisely in the same manner, and the whole of that scene of painful mockery presented itself strongly before him. He remained absorbed in gloomy reverie; a chilling doubt, a secret discontent, clung, in spite of all his efforts, to his thoughts. Why should he be denied the enjoyment of the best, the purest affections of his being? The ideas, if not the words, of our sublime Milton were present to his mind; and he felt, for the first time, a secret abhorrence of those hypocrites who " austerely talk,"—

> " Defaming as impure, what God declares
> Pure; and, commands to some, leaves free to all."

He felt, that to this ill-judged attempt to force our imperfect nature on too lofty a pinnacle, was owing its disgraceful fall among the class of men to which he belonged. Such an impracticable elevation, he began to regard as a sort of spiritual Babel, which, like the Babel of yore, lay crushed in its own weakness, folly, and presumption.

Augustus heard the heavy carriages thunder, one after another, through the paved archway; the trampling and neighing of horses, an occasional note of music, or a peal of laughter met his ear. On a sudden, however, these sounds ceased; an unusual stillness reigned around, and, somewhat startled by the contrast, Augustus raised his head from the folds of his robe. He thought his clerical companions seemed surprised; distant doors were banging, and footsteps were hurrying to and fro; several menials, pale and alarmed, looked into the chapel and disappeared. At length came the sound of many voices, in rage and lamentation; a crowd seemed approaching the chapel; the voices, mingled and confused, grew every moment louder, till the Count rushed in like a madman, gnashing his teeth and tearing his hair, followed by the Baron of Elsenheim, his sons, and several other noblemen, all trying in vain to appease him.

At the proper time the bride had been sought for in the oratory; two hours had elapsed, and it was no longer possible to conceal that there was no bride to be found.

The scene that ensued baffles description. Augustus at length, partly by force, partly by entreaty, succeeded in conveying his brother home. The wondering guests slowly dispersed. The Baron, with the female part of his family, shut himself up; while his sons and vassals scoured the surrounding country, threatening vengeance and destruction to the unhappy girl, and all who might be concerned in her flight.

Wilhelmina was pointed out by Emmeline's sisters as an object of suspicion; and to her cottage did the brothers first direct their steps. She had already returned from the castle, whither she had gone, arrayed in all her finery, to assist at the toilet of the bride. They found her seated on the floor, sobbing and crying bitterly. She steadily disclaimed all knowledge of Emmeline's intentions, who, she allowed, had visited her of late more frequently than usual; but it was her habit never to pass her cottage, upon any occasion, without doing so. She said she had observed that Emmeline *looked* melancholy, but had never heard her express any aversion to her approaching marriage; and when she (Wilhelmina) spoke of it in terms of joy and pride, she had never been checked by Emmeline. She unhesitatingly denied having seen her on the close of the previous day. This was all that Wilhelmina could or would reveal. Strict search was made within and about her cottage, but in vain.

Augustus delayed as long as possible his departure to Suabia, partly to console and support his brother, partly in the hope that a short time might discover the retreat of Emmeline, and that he might act as mediator between her and her family, trusting, at least, to ameliorate the severity of her punishment. This for others; but in his own bosom he carefully locked up feelings far more acute even than those he sought to console. He acquitted himself, it is true, of ever having in word, in look, or even in thought, encouraged the love of Emmeline; that love, so full of truth and of despair, which, in despite of obstacles utterly insurmountable, had seemed to grow with her growth, and strengthen with her strength; that love, for which all worldly blessings, amply as they were showered on her head, had been rejected, and for which she was now a houseless and desolate wanderer! Where was she? what had become of her? Could he imagine that young and delicate form condemned to want and labor? or had it found a lingering death in the depth of some concealed cave? or been dashed from the brow of the precipice? or did it lie congealed in the mountain torrent? Alas! how willingly would he have braved the scorn of the world, and the severe injunctions of his religious creed—all that till then he had dreaded, or held inviolable—to have wrung from her tresses the cold dews of night—to have warmed her on his heart—to have given his love for her love, his life for her life!

To all but him, the event was as inexplicable as it was astounding: he alone held a clue, slight, but certain, to the desperate step she had taken. In the inmost recesses of the woods, and along the lonely margins of the lakes he called upon her name; and, surrounded by their gloomy solitude, gave way to the heart-rending grief, which, from the eyes of his fellow-men, he was forced to conceal.

At times, he almost hoped that Heaven had taken her to itself. "What would it avail her to be found? My brother's love is turned to gall; her very mother would refuse even a tear to her supplications; and if she took refuge with me, she would find in my arms but disgrace and misery, without the power even of protecting her against the vengeance of her family, and the offended laws of her country. No, Emmeline! thy pure and suffering spirit has fled where it will find pardon and peace! I have but a little time yet to struggle on, and then shall we meet where it is no crime to love!"

A few weeks passed away, and, by degrees, all hope of recovering the lost Emmeline, or of ascertaining her fate, was given up. Her eldest brother, Rudolph, a harsh and haughty man, had already departed for the wars in Suabia; whither Augustus became now exceedingly anxious, according to his orders, to repair. The brothers, therefore, parted: Augustus, accompanied by a numerous armed train, to Ulm; and the Count to Vienna, where he hoped, amid gaieties and pomp, and above all, by a suitable marriage, to heal the wound that had been inflicted on his love and his pride.

Augustus found Suabia even in a worse state than he had apprehended. The peasants were, in all directions, rising *en masse*; and the imperial army, though brave and well-disciplined, was, owing to the poverty of Charles V., small, and ill-supplied. It is not necessary to remind our readers, that the priesthood, at that time, not only influenced the councils of armies, but often personally engaged in their contests.

The zeal, energy, and ability of Augustus, joined to the unbounded confidence placed in him, rendered his presence of much importance. About a month after his arrival, a desperate conflict took place near Ulm, in which the Imperialists were successful; but, while in pursuit of the flying peasantry, a body of the latter suddenly rallied, and discharged the few fire-arms they possessed. Augustus received a wound in the shoulder, sufficiently severe to prevent his proceeding; his horse, at the same time, being killed under him. Unwilling, however, to draw a single follower from the pursuit, he retired to the bank of a small, clear stream, where he attempted to stanch the blood and bind the wound; but heat, fatigue, and over-excitement, had done their work, and he fell, exhausted, without being able even to refresh himself by a draught of the water that bubbled past him.

On recovering, he found himself supported by some one who was bathing his temples and the palms of his hands, and who, on seeing him able to bear it, applied himself with great skill, coolness, and delicacy of touch, to the dressing of the wound. Augustus looked up and beheld a thin, pale boy, apparently not more than twelve or thirteen years of age, and arrayed as a page, but by no means handsomely. When he had finished dressing the wound, he gave his patient a draught of the cool water; and making him up a pillow of moss, assisted him to lie down, covered him with his military cloak, and then went to the road-side to watch for some of his returning followers.

The first demand Augustus made, when awakening on his own bed at Ulm, was for the stranger-boy who had so providentially succored him, and, perhaps, had been the means of saving his life. The boy was immediately brought forward; and Augustus, dismissing those about him, inquired who he was.

"I am," replied the youth, "the son of Wilhelmina, a vassal of your brother, the count; but who has resided on the lands of the baron of Elsenheim, since she nursed my foster-sister, the Lady Emmeline."

"Indeed!" exclaimed Augustus, with great interest; "you are the son of Wilhelmina! But, how came you here? I thought you were in the train of the young Ulric of Elsenheim."

"I was so," replied the boy; "but my mother felt herself affronted at the suspicion cast upon her by the family, on the occasion of the Lady Emmeline's disappearance, and she has gone back to Altenberg. She had also sent me word (for she cannot write) to quit the Lord Ulric, to make the best of my way to Ulm, where I should find you, and to proffer you my services, as to the brother of my liege lord. I have had a weary travel all the way from ———; but, thank Heaven, I came in good time!"

"Undraw that window-curtain a little, and let me look at you." The boy did as he was ordered. "I forget your name."

"Theodore, my lord."

"Poor boy! you do, indeed, look worn out and fatigued! You appear younger than your foster-sister."

"Yet we are, as near as may be, the same age."

"She is taller than you are."

"No, my lord, we are about the same height; but a lad of sixteen will hardly look so old, or so tall, as a young lady of that age."

"True," replied Augustus, thoughtfully, with his eye still fixed on the youth.

"I have been considered," continued Theodore, coloring a little and drawing himself up, "to resemble the Lady Emmeline. My mother was very proud of that resemblance, slight as it was, and made everybody remark it; but I fear you, my lord, do not discover it, I am now so much altered for the worse."

"Yes; I think there is a likeness, though I am scarcely a judge, (and Augustus sighed deeply,) as I have only seen the Lady Emmeline once, for a few minutes, during the last two years. Your hair and complexion are darker and the slight resemblance you bear will wear off as you grow up and get more manly."

"I am sorry for it," said Theodore, looking a little disconcerted; at which trait of youthful vanity Augustus could not repress a smile.

He liked the frank, yet modest and simple manner of the boy so much, that he took him at once into his service as page; and, although his want of birth would prevent his rising higher, it would be easy, he thought, to provide for him in a few years, in some other department of the household. Theodore accordingly was, to his great apparent delight, soon arrayed in the handsome and becoming, but somewhat fanciful dress of a page, in those times. He looked so well in it, and a few days' rest had made so favorable an alteration in his appearance, that the resemblance of which he had boasted, began to strike Augustus more forcibly, and secretly influenced him further to notice and favor the boy. He was timid, gentle, and apparently in delicate health; his habits were exceedingly reserved; and when not with his master, he would retire into the little room assigned him, and would there read, write, or practice on his lute— an instrument on which he excelled, and which, he said, he loved, because his dear young Lady Emmeline had herself given him his first lessons. The sound of the war-trumpet made him turn pale; but he was remarkably prompt and skillful in attending to the wounded. Augustus, in his hours of rest and relaxation at home, was never without Theodore, whose cheerful smile, interesting and intelligent conversation, lute and song, only awaited a glance from his master, to whom he soon became as a young and cherished brother. Placed on a stool at his feet, even when Augustus was occupied in writing, or in deep thought, or in conversation with others, would lean his head unreproved upon his knee, and look at or listen to him with that affectionate devotion, that mixture of love and veneration, we feel for a beneficent and superior being.

At first, the name of the Lady Emmeline was sometimes naturally on the lips of Theodore, but it always produced an expression of so much pain on the countenance of Augustus, that the page, apparently presuming he had not recovered from the indignity his brother, the Count, had received, forbore to dwell upon it.

Rudolph of Elsenheim, the eldest brother of Emmeline, had also taken up his winter quarters in Ulm. A civil, but distant intercourse, took place between him and Augustus; for, among other ill-effects of the strange event that had occurred, the alienation of the two families could scarcely be prevented. Twice, on the occasion of a ceremonious visit made by Rudolph, Theodore effected his escape in much agitation; for which Augustus rather reproved him: " You need not be alarmed; you and your mother are our vassals; and your having been so long in the service of the Elsenheims, was a matter of courtesy on our part, and not of right on theirs."

The winter months were passing away, during which the Imperialists had received great reinforcements; and it was confidently expected, that early in the spring the insurrection of Suabia would be annihilated.

Affairs were in this situation, when, on the occasion of a great church-festival, at which Augustus was to preside, he, for the first time, pressed Theodore to accompany him.

" You have hitherto," observed Augustus, " pleaded delicacy of health, and the effect of cold in church, as excuses for not attending its service; but your health now is quite restored; for I can scarcely recognize," continued Augustus, smiling, " the thin, pale boy, that tended me so providentially by the riverside; and you well know, Theodore, how almost rigid I am in the discipline of my household, and how much I insist upon their strict observance, both of public and private worship."

" I am ready to attend you, my lord," replied the boy, meekly, but dejectedly, " at high mass this evening."

The church was magnificently ornamented and illuminated; and the celebration of mass, in the absence of the bishop, devolved on Augustus. Great numbers of all classes of people were present. Among the nobles who stood near the railings of the altar, Augustus remarked, not only Rudolph of Elsenheim, but also his younger brother Ulric, who, it seems, must have just arrived; and their numerous followers, easily known by their badge, were dispersed about the church. The same was the case with the armed followers of Augustus; but his household stood together, and among these was placed Theodore. Augustus could not help remarking, in the intervals of the ceremony, that the looks of the two brothers were fixed on himself with a peculiar expression; it partook of scorn, triumph, and revenge. He felt surprised, and occasionally in his turn, looked full at them with his dark, stern, and penetrating eyes; but they did not quail beneath his gaze; and a sort of contemptuous smile, at such moments, slightly curled their lips. Their looks were never moved from off him, except to settle on his household group; to which Augustus also directed his. Theodore was almost hid behind the ample cloak of the seneschal, and seemed scarcely able to support himself. Not far from the brothers, and wearing their badge, stood a fine, dark, sturdy youth, whose looks were also often fixed upon the same group, with an uneasy and almost terrified expression.

" There is some mystery," thought Augustus, " hanging over that boy, Theodore; I am convinced he has left the Elsenheims without leave, and has cajoled me with falsehoods. This accounts for the whole of his singular conduct; but, before I sleep, I will know the truth."

After the service, Augustus retired into the vestry, to unrobe, and was a little surprised to find that Theodore, who had come to the church with him, was not among the attendants who remained to escort him home. It appeared that he had already departed with the rest of the household.

In honor of the festival, the streets were lighted, and the houses mostly opened for the reception of company; many gay scenes, and sounds of music and merriment, caught the eye and ear of Augustus, but he anxiously proceeded homeward. His saloon was also lighted, and a few clerical visitors were assembled, whom he managed to dismiss as soon as possible. He then inquired for Theodore, and was told that he had appeared unwell the whole evening, and had retired to his room immediately on his return home; and also that there was a young man just arrived, who anxiously begged permission to speak with the page. " Should he be admitted ? "

" Certainly," replied Augustus; and, in another instant, the young follower of the Elsenheims, whom Augustus had observed at church, was ushered in.

" You wish to speak to my page ? "

" If you please, my lord."

" You may do so; but I have my reasons for being present at your conference. Follow me."

The young man did so unhesitatingly; and Augustus proceeded to Theodore's room, and as he opened the door, the stranger rushed by him, and hurriedly addressed the page: " My poor mother is dead, and, on her death-bed, confessed all—all! Fly, for Heaven's sake ! You are in the utmost danger ! Delay not a moment ! I give you this warning at the hazard of my life ! "

Then, turning, he was about to escape from the room, when the athletic grasp of Augustus seized him.

" Who are you ? " he asked, in a voice of thunder.

The boy struggled to free himself, while he answered, " I am Theodore, Wilhelmina's son ! "

" And this ? " said Augustus, pointing to the page.

" Oh, my lord! there is no time for jesting," replied the true Theodore, " when every instant increases the danger of the Lady Emmeline ! "

Augustus let go his hold, and the boy was down the stairs and out of the house in an instant.

With strangely mingled feelings of the keenest joy and the deepest despair, Augustus closed the door and approached the yet motionless form of Emmeline. She suddenly retreated.

"Come not near me! For the sake of Heaven have pity on me, unworthy as I am!"

"Emmeline!" he replied, with a look and voice replete with tenderness, "misjudge me not; deem me not so undeserving of all thy love, thy sacrifices and thy sufferings! Confide in me! would to Heaven thou hadst done so sooner!"

As he spoke, he unclasped the light mantle which he wore. "Let me wrap you in this, and I will convey you to a subterranean passage, where you will be safe for a few hours. My people shall be on guard for the night, and, by early dawn, some scheme shall be matured for your future concealment."

"For my concealment," replied Emmeline, pleadingly, "but not—not for my separation *from you!*"

"No, my love—*my wife!*" whispered the now entirely subdued Augustus, as he impressed on her lips one long and fervent kiss; "*God hath joined us together, and no man shall put us asunder!*"

Alas! were not these the words of impiety?

He carefully wrapped her in the mantle, and, lifting her in his arms, prepared to convey her to her retreat.

The emotions of the last few moments had been so overwhelming, that neither Augustus nor Emmeline had heeded a low and peculiar murmur of voices, nor the sound of advancing footsteps. Before they themselves had reached the door of the apartment, it was flung open, and the two brothers of Emmeline, armed to the teeth, with about twenty followers and a civil magistrate stood before them. It was the work of a moment for Augustus to spring back with his trembling burden, place himself against the opposite wall, draw a double-edged poniard from his girdle, and stand on his defence.

"All here are friends and brothers," said the magistrate; "let there be no blood shed, but the blood of our enemies! My lord Augustus of Altenberg, resign to the legal authority of her family, the unhappy and misguided girl, who now seeks shelter in thy arms!"

"Never!" replied Augustus, "but with my heart's blood!"

At that moment he heard, to his great relief, the gathering of his household, and the advance of such followers as the only esquire, who was at home on this festival-night could collect. Augustus never allowed a sentinel about his house, and this irruption had been made so boldly, yet so very quietly, that it had completely succeeded.

"On your guard!" said Ulric to his men; who immediately faced to the landing-place, to receive those who were ascending the steps to the attack.

"Yield her thou hypocrite!" exclaimed the infuriated Rudolph, waving his sword and gnashing his teeth.

"I will never yield her!" was the reply. "On! on! my brave fellows, to the rescue! Cut down these night-marauders—these cowardly house breakers!"

A cheering shout from his advancing followers without, answered this appeal. The clash of arms and the yell of the meeting foes were heard.

"Then, priest, thy blood be on thine own head!" And, as Rudolph spoke, he drew, and fired a pistol full at Augustus; but rage and confusion had caused his hand to waver. Emmeline made a sudden bound in the arms of her protector; he felt a warm torrent gush over his breast, and he heard the cries of "You have killed her—your sister!" The strong spring of his mind gave way; images of darkness, streaked with flames and blood, danced before him; for a moment he was mad, and the next he was insensible.

It was midnight: the tumult had ceased; not a step was heard, save those of the guard who patrolled the street; every window and door in the terrified neighborhood had been closed, and a melancholy calm had succeeded to the fury of the affray.

"He is recovering!" said the physician, anxiously bending over the yet inanimate form of Augustus.

"Thank Heaven!" was repeated from lip to lip of the many who were watching him. The eyes of their master opened heavily; but, after a pause, he started up, and looked wildly round; then, clasping his hands on his forehead, remained quite motionless for a few minutes; at length he slowly withdrew them, raised his head, and, looking at the leech, asked in a low, firm tone, "Is she dead?"

The physician bowed his head, without reply.

"And the body?" he inquired, calmly.

"We would not, my lord," answered an esquire, "permit the body to be removed from hence without your permission. When the ruffians found what they had done, they retreated, almost without striking another blow."

"Where is she?"

"My lord," said the physician, "the body has been well cared for by the seneschal's wife and daughter; and prayers will presently be said over it."

"Lead me to her chamber!"

"Pray, let us dissuade you, my dear lord!" pleadingly repeated several voices.

"Peace, and obey me!" He attempted to rise; they assisted him. "Order the women to leave the chamber, and let none intrude while I am there." And in a few minutes, Augustus was alone with the dead.

The couch had been drawn to the centre of the little room, and a few lights had been placed round it; from the pavement had been carefully erased all marks of the contest. The body lay shrouded in linen, white as snow, from which it was scarcely to be distinguished in complexion; the women had, with melancholy pride, laid out every long, bright tress, and in the folded hands were placed a few winter-flowers: the face was beautifully placid: she looked as if about to awaken with a smile.

> "So fair, so calm, so softly sealed,
> The first, last look, by death revealed."

He bent over her, and touched with his lips the serene and virginal brow.

"O maiden!" he murmured, "how deep, how faithful, how pure, has been thine ill-requited love! how enduring, and yet how hopeless! tried by thy suffering, and sealed with thy blood! Is such, indeed, the love of woman? Pray for me, thou martyred saint; and the union which has been denied to us on earth, will be granted in Heaven! If, here, our love contracted aught of sin, may all that remains of my life be accepted as an atonement; then will I follow thee, my own, my loved, my murdered Emmeline!"

His grief, for a moment, lost its calmness, and a few burning tears forced their way. He lifted up one of those lovely and motionless locks of hair, severed it with his poniard, and placed it in his bosom; then stooped again to press her lips, but started from them in horror—how icy chill! Where was the fragrance, the warmth, the life, the love, with which, in a first, last kiss, they had met his a few hours before? He retreated; one look—one long, long look—and he was gone.

Augustus of Altenberg was never seen from that hour. It was supposed that he made use of his knowledge of the subterranean passage to effect his escape.

In two months after, a letter was received by the emperor, (who much regretted his loss,) and one by his brother, the Count of Altenberg, detailing, exactly, the circumstances that had occurred. Augustus evidently considered such an explanation due to the memory of Emmeline, and to his own.

By Wilhelmina's death-bed confession, it appeared, that it was not until the evening before the intended marriage with the Count of Altenberg, that she was at last induced to yield to the supplications of Emmeline, to assist her in her concealment and flight; had she done so sooner, Emmeline would not have delayed her disappearance till the day fixed for her marriage. Wilhelmina declared that nothing could have induced her to comply, had she not been under the conviction that Emmeline would have put an end to her existence, rather than become the wife of the Count.

About half a century from the time these events occurred, on the removal of a monastery of La Trappe, by the command of De Rance, the regenerator of that order, a grave, apart from all the others, marked by a rough stone, was observed: on the stone, the name of "Augustus" was rudely carved.

Mrs. HARRIET E. FURMAN.

THE subject of this obituary was a grand-daughter of Mr. Moses Stone. It may be gratifying to her friends, and to those of her mother, who was a native of Mount Auburn, to peruse this testimony of love and respect to her memory.

"Blessed are the dead who die in the Lord."

These words sometimes come to us with peculiar freshness and force, as if the voice from Heaven were speaking to us, instead of the beloved disciple—as if we took the words from the mouth of the Lord, instead of the printed page. So it seemed as we stood by the cold but consecrated clay of our dead friend and sister in Christ, Harriet Emeline Furman, wife of Rev. Charles E. Furman, who died in the city of Rochester, N. Y., recently. Mrs. Furman was born in Hallowell, Maine, in 1809. When about four years old, her parents removed to Portland, and became members of Dr. Payson's church, by whom she was baptized, and under whom she received all her early religious training. In 1827 the family came to Rochester, and in 1830, during the powerful revivals then in progress, she gave herself to the Lord, and united with the Brick Church. She was married the next Winter, and removed to Clarkson, of which church her husband was then pastor. Noble in presence and dignified in manner, she commanded at once the respect and esteem of all ; and these invariably grew into affection as she became better known. She was punctual in the discharge of every Christian duty, and yet she did it for duty's sake—shrinking from every honor which the ladies sought to confer upon her, and with characteristic meekness and modestly taking the humblest place.

As an instance of this punctuality I may mention the fact, that during the thirty years of her married life, she never entered the sanctuary after the services had commenced. And in this respect she ordered her household after her, requiring the same punctuality from them : and that nothing might be in their way, never retiring on Saturday night until all her arrangements for the Sabbath were completed. The public services of the Sabbath over, all necessary domestic duties of the day done, she gathered her children about her to read the Scriptures, teach them the catechism and study the lesson for the next Lord's Day. But she did not confine her labors to her household. She thought of those who were without, and especially those for whose soul no man cares. She thought of them on her death bed; and almost the only thing she asked of her husband, was the promise to labor for the spiritual welfare of some who to her were perfect strangers. The congregations of Clarkson, Victor, and Medina, where she and her most estimable husband lived and labored, owe her a great debt of love, greater even than they suppose, for much that her husband performed, she prompted. In neither of these places did she leave an enemy behind. There are no grudges to bury in the grave.

About a year and a half since, her health, which had been uniformly good, began to fail, and it was evident from the first that the disease was mortal. Most of the time her sufferings seemed almost beyond the power of human endurance, but her patience never gave out. Not an impatient or fretful word escaped her lips, and it will be a pleasant memory among so many painful ones, that she never was permitted to hear one. Like her Lord, she thought more of others than herself, and often said it was harder for her husband and the children to see her suffer and die than for her to suffer and die. When her devoted daughter, in one of those strains, into which love is so often brought, would ask : "Mother, what can we do to relieve you?" she meekly replied : "*You will have to let me die ; that is to be my relief.*"

When her last hour came, it brought no darkness; how could it when it brought her Lord? "I am as well prepared to die," she said, "as I ever shall be, for all my trust is in my Redeemer." Without a groan or sigh she fell asleep. Her works praise her, her life is her eulogium, and her epitaph is written on many a grateful heart. "I heard a voice from Heaven saying unto me, Write, Blessed are the dead which die in the Lord, from henceforth; yea, saith the Spirit, that they may rest from their labors, and their works do follow them."

J. B. R.

THE EVERLASTING MEMORIAL.

BY REV. HORATIUS BONAR, D. D.

Up and away, like the dew of the morning,
 Soaring from earth to its home in the sun;
So let me steal away, gently and lovingly,
 Only remembered by what I have done.

My name, and my place, and my tomb all forgotten,
 The brief race of time well and patiently run,
So let me pass away, peacefully, silently,
 Only remembered by what I have done.

Up and away! like the odors of sunset,
 That sweeten the twilight as darkness comes on;
So be my life—a thing felt, but not noticed,
 And I but remembered by what I have done.

Yes, like the fragrance that wanders in freshness
 When the flowers it came from are closed up and gone,
So would I be to this world's weary dwellers—
 Only remembered by what I have done.

Needs there the praise of the love-written record,
 The name and the epitaph graved on the stone?
The things we have lived for, let them be our story,
 We but remembered by what we have done.

I need not be missed; if my life has been bearing
 (As its summer and autumn moved silently on),
The bloom and the fruit, and the seed of its season,
 I shall still be remembered by what I have done.

I need not be missed: if another succeed me,
 To reap down those fields which in spring I have sown,

He who ploughed and who sowed is not missed by the reaper,
He is only remembered by what he has done.

Not myself, but the truth that in life I have spoken,
For myself, but the seed that in life I have sown,
Shall pass on to ages—all about me forgotten,
Save the truth I have spoken, the things I have done.

So let my living be, so be my dying—
So let my name be unblazoned, unknown—
Unpraised and unmissed, I shall yet be remembered;
Yes, but remembered by what I have done.

CHURCHYARDS AND EPITAPHS.

IT has happened to be my fortune to live during the summer months in the near neighborhood of one of the London cemeteries, within range of the odors of the roses, the mignonette, and other flowers that sustain by their presence there, thoughts of beauty and hope in the minds of those who choose to wander among the gravestones. Close to London it is pleasant and soothing to compare this tranquil, ornate ground with those which disfigure and disgrace the great town.

In various directions round London, as estates change hands and conveniences occur, pieces of spacious ground fall into the possession of societies. Yew trees, willow trees speckle them, encircle them. Temples are erected, and due consecration performed, that those whose creeds are different, may each have for his remains the form of rite which his fathers professed. Groups of children, knots of decorous wanderers may be seen strolling in the sunshine, among grass, and trees, and flowers. To such a place the new summer brings its fresh revival of beauty, as it does to the garden or the forest.

In strolling through a country churchyard, who does not stop to read the records?—and how profoundly natural it is! The instinct of humanity draws you to the grave's foot; the thought stirring in you, what experience the departed has had different from yours, how long he lived, even. A trivial little fact about him will set you musing; a reflection, there, that seems generally to embody his sentiments or experience, will linger in your memory like music. How far are epitaphs liable to what we call criticism? How far can the law be laid down regarding writings of such a peculiar and exceptional character? An epitaph is strictly a publication. This, which seems so obvious, is really the most neglected consideration possible. An epitaph publishes itself in open sunshine to all the world; and, indeed, has a far better chance of being read, than one book out of every five hundred. It professes always to inform, to instruct, to warn, to describe. It is one of those things which everybody thinks himself competent to compose; yet a good epitaph is the rarest thing in literature.

To begin with: what should be our idea of an epitaph? The name implies, in its simplicity, an inscription on a tomb. That idea implies the preservation of the memory of the dead. From the builder of a funeral pyramid to the erector of a wooden plank supported by two posts in a country churchyard, all such architects have the memory of the dead person in view. But there are infinite varieties of worth, and character, and adventure, and importance, to be recorded; and the epitaph soon becomes a portion of literature. The Scandinavian chief in one age has his place of rest indicated by a huge mound; a thousand years later, a similar hero of the same race is laid in a cathedral, and his memory is preserved in writing. Intellectual culture has become the supreme honor since his day; so, his memory owes its celebrity to the literary record of it. Hence, the epitaph of the great man will be no common composition. Hence, it has been felt that pre-eminent worth should be recorded in language of dignity and excellence, to express the harmony between the eminence achieved, and the culture of the age which records its admiration of it.

It is, therefore, natural that the epitaph should become in time, somewhat elaborated. A simple, rude people see in the mound of this great man a symbol of his greatness that strikes at once on the imagination. The wanderer from a distant part of the province sees it, and feels the same. There is little communication between distant people in these ages. In a cultivated age, what is written of the great man serves the mound's purpose. It is present to the popular imagination everywhere. Thus, a good modern epitaph on a great man ought to be the very essence of all the literature of his time will say about him; something to circulate in a compact form, like his likeness on a medal. Let me give examples of what I mean. Does not Dr. Johnson beautifully describe Goldsmith's felicity of natural genius, when he says, that he "touched nothing which he did not adorn?" Or, look at the line on Franklin: "He snatched the lightning from Heaven, and the sceptre from kings." This is the poetry of his life's actions in a line. If posterity, again, knew nothing of Ben Jonson but that somebody expressed the general feeling about him, by "O rare Ben Jonson," they would carry away a capital idea of him. These are strict epitaphs. You cannot write a detailed narrative of a man's exploits and character on his tombstone. Neither, in the case of a notable man, is it needful. But it is right and natural that the place where his bones lie should have an appropriate inscription. The epitaph gathers, as it were, the very honey out of the flowers that compose his crown, and gives it to the world. So, to my mind, the writer of a fine epitaph not only does a graceful literary performance, but does a service of importance to the world. It is impossible to calculate the good done to society at large, by the circulation of brief, terse sayings, carrying wisdom in them. And if wisdom is in its place any where, surely it is on a monument. An epitaph which preserves a man's memory embalmed in its beauty, should be written with the care and reverence becoming the spot and the object for which it is intended.

OUR OLD SCHOOLHOUSE.

I LOVE to cherish those hallowed memories which cluster around the scenes of my child-life. I delight to summon up the many-tinted pictures of the past,—

> " Painted by Memory's pen,
> On life's fast-fading page,"

and feel their softening and subduing influence on my mind. It thrills some of the soul's holier chords, which the almost ceaseless rush of later-life will hardly ever cause to vibrate. The walk in the forest, when the south wind stole gently through the thick branches, and the fleckered pavement of sunlight and shade danced so lightly on the green moss at our feet; the little brook on whose banks we spent many hours of childhood's unconscious gaiety, discovering beauties and feeling joys which we never more can see or feel; the autumn excursions in pursuit of nuts, gathered for the long winter evenings which flew so joyously by, when the loved family circle were gathered at the home fireside; the roguish sports of winter, amid snow-drifts and ice-fields; the kind, parental counsels, mingled, perhaps, with a mother's tears and a father's prayers ;—remembrances of all these, and many a bright vision besides, awaken very pleasing emotions in the heart, not too deeply corroded with life's cares.

But from all the recollections of earlier scenes, I would single my school-days as among the happiest and most profitable. I doubt whether any period of life is so fruitful in unalloyed pleasure as those years usually spent in the common district school. There are griefs, to be sure, but they hardly come ere they fade away—tears soon give place to smiles. Many bright memories linger around the place of those early joys, and "our old schoolhouse" tells them almost all.

The building in which I first thumbed Webster's spelling-book crowns a high eminence, which we youngsters used to denominate the "hill of science." Many and many a time have we climbed the real hill, but how far we ever ascended the ideal one, I will not attempt to say. At any rate, we sometimes considered ourselves—

> " Above the common walks of life : "

for we could look down in every direction. Still, we loved the spot. Tier upon tier of hazy hills were piled in the dim distance, sometimes almost blending with the blue sky beyond. The lightest summer breeze brought to us its burden of fragrance. Birds sang us sweet songs, and flowers bloomed brightly along our path. Even in winter, when fierce gales swept by in all their fury, we saw some scenes of grandeur and beauty.

But its summer robes were the glory of our hill-top. When the soft sunlight and gentle rains of opening spring dressed it in living green, we rejoiced.

When fleecy clouds lay almost motionless in the blue dome above, and scarce a breeze fluttered by, we loved it,—loved to gambol on its sides, and gaze into the misty distance. I seem to see, even now, the joyous groups of the past flitting lightly over the broad green, and to hear again the ringing of their laughter. As in days gone by, the single old oak yet serves as a green canopy for childhood's sports. Long ago—

> " We played domestic duties in its shade,
> Feigned age and winter in surrounding June,
> Held mock tribunals, tried each manly trade,
> And lived whole life-times in a single noon."

Many of the old land-marks are gone, but memory preserves them all : and all are celebrated in the lay of a poet-pupil, whose words I have just quoted.

" Our old schoolhouse," incomplete as it is, marred and disfigured by the varied impress of rising genius, is dear to me. Many-toned voices seem issuing from its walls, speaking of the past. They call up reminiscences of former teachers. . . . . They speak, too, of many other true teachers, who nobly and earnestly labored for our good, who sought by word and deed, to guide us in wisdom's way. May Heaven's richest blessings be theirs. But in milder tones and softer accents they speak of the gentle lady who several summers presided there. I was very young, then, but never shall I forget the winning ways, and mild words, and kindly deeds of that teacher. We all loved her. We longed for her approbation, and the little mementoes she gave were cherished keepsakes. That smiling face was like sunlight to the young hearts of her charge, and its gleams still linger there. Death early marked her as its victim, and called her to the land " where angels dwell." But though dead, she yet speaks. Her monument is in the hearts of her pupils. I doubt not that her influence is felt to-day in many a mind.

Still other voices come from those time-worn walls, telling of the bands that used daily to gather there. Each vacant seat is eloquent. Even those rough carvings tell their own story of youthful faults and foibles. Through that open window we watched the approach of our teacher. On that bench we recited our daily lessons, and what memories cluster around the place ! Here we studied, and there we played—here we laughed, and there we wept. I know of no spot more prolific in remembrances than this school-room, nor of stronger friendships than were sometimes formed there. I am young yet, but a few years have brought changes. The groups of yesterday, to-day are scattered. Some have wandered far from home, and a few gone " over the river."

Yet memory re-unites them all in the old, familiar spot, and fancy weaves bright pictures of past realities.

The long " noon-time," with its record of merry sports, now comes up. I see again the bare-footed and sun-browned urchins, intent in the mysteries of " hide and seek." I mingle once more with loved school-mates in the exciting games of " blind man's buff," or " I spy." Down this path we walked in by-gone days, after green boughs and fresh flowers to decorate our schoolroom

Along that sunny slope we listened to the humming of the bee, plucked wild honeysuckles and clover, watched the bright-winged butterfly, or talked of childhood's joys and griefs. Here was our "mud well," and there our stone-fenced "play-house." Under that spreading tree, when tired of our gambols, we flung ourselves on the green turf, and toying with the "wish-grass" built those mammoth "air-castles" which later years have toppled over.

All these old pathways grow fresh again, as memory travels back, and all are freighted with some good lesson from the past. I love them all, and wherever I may wander in coming years, I never shall forget the joyous recollections connected with "OUR OLD SCHOOLHOUSE."

HOW LONG!

BY MRS. J. H. HANAFORD.

(A young lady, with dying breath, exclaimed, "How long, dear Saviour, oh, how long!" Her exclamation has suggested the following lines.)

How long before the pearly gates
    Shall open wide to me,
How long before my barque shall reach
    Eternity's broad sea,
How long, dear Saviour! ere my heart
    Shall thril! at sight of thee?

How long before the precious ones,
    Who left me sighing here,
Shall greet my weary, hastening feet,
    And Jesus say, "Draw near,"
While from my grief-dimmed eyes he wipes
    Away each earth-born tear!

How long must I the conflict wage
    With foes without, within,
How long before I'll stand complete,
    In Heaven, without sin,
And greet the cherished ones of earth
    Who earlier entered in!

How long before the golden bowl
    Will break beside the fount,
And I to lofty heights of bliss
    Forevermore shall mount,
And joy, through all the countless years,
    Thy mercy to recount!

Not long, dear Lord! I hear thy voice,
    Thou whisp'rest, " Come to me,"—
Farewell, O earth, and earth's beloved!
    Saviour, I rise to thee,
With loving, wise, and holy souls
    Forevermore to be.

Beverly, 1861.

A SUMMER RHAPSODY.

BY JOHN INMAN.

AWAY to the mountain side, and the dark rapid stream of my own native Cabarras! I am weary of toil, and the conventions of city life, and the prison wall of thousands of human eyes, that are ever upon me; I would be free once more, as I was free in the days that have long past away—on the lone hill—by the still lake, set like a sparkling stone, in the very heart of a forest whose tall pines have bowed, with their eternal green branches, to the winds of a hundred years—or still farther away from the haunts of mankind, to the vast prairie that stretches, miles upon miles, with no hillock, or tree, not even a shrub on which the eye may repose for a moment, as it sweeps the level horizon. I pant for solitude, and room to give way to my own thoughts; for a world where there is no artifice; where there is none to do or receive injury, or for whose sake I must subdue the fresh-spring impulses of my own nature. In the crowded city my actions are not of my own guiding; my course is governed by something out of myself, for wherever I turn, there is a barrier of mode, or of prejudice, or of factitious propriety, not founded upon the unchangeable basis of nature, and reason, and free thought, but upon solemn devices of little rectangular minds that move only by precedent; better to stand still for ever, than walk in a path not marked out by mine own will, and with eyes forbidden to wander at large over the distant landscape, to the mountain that buries its head in the clouds, or far away to the depths of the blue arch overhead, lest my feet turn aside for a moment, out of the beaten track in which every step is controlled by the presence of thousands. This is not the life of a man; of that wonderful being whose mind was intended to rule over all the material world and be governed alone by its inherent unshackled energies; in this world of system and regulation, the soul is stripped of its privilege; it is no longer an agent, but like the needle surrounded with iron, reft of its power and constantly forced into directions adverse to its nature.

But away to the desert! my spirit longs for the free solitude of the uninhabited wild, where the herbage has sprung from the rich soil, and shot up to luxuriance, and withered away at the summer's close, year after year for ages, and never bent under a human footstep; where the destroyer has never come with his accursed inventions to take the innocent life of the fearless bird, or the fleet deer that starts not with the wisdom of dear-bought experience from the fatal presence of man; where the glorious forest trees have never been swept from the earth by thousands to gratify human caprice or human cupidity. Let me forget the world of constraint, and sorrow, and toil, and perpetual artifice, and escape for a time to the regions of nature and liberty, where only God's hand has wrought in unspeakable wonders; the region amid whose glories I revel in dreams.

Behold! ay, gaze forever in mute admiration! Wheresoever I turn, there is matter for breathless, fearful delight. The fierce rays of noon are scorching the earth, but not one can pierce the dark canopy under whose shade I stand. These pines are the growth of a hundred years; their huge trunks, blackened by age, and straight as the arrow whose strongest flight could hardly attain their summits, tower aloft like the pillars of some vast temple, measured by whose stupendous dimensions the proudest of human fabrics would appear mean and diminutive. Egyptian or Grecian art never imagined a roof of such lofty and solemn grandeur as that formed by the dense unbroken mass of their gloomy verdure. There is not a breath of air to rustle among their wide spreading branches; and nothing disturbs the awful quiet, save now and then the quick, angry bark of the squirrel, the busy tap of the strong-billed woodpecker, or the harsh scream of the mocking-bird. The soul is weighed down with a feeling of reverence, and bows to the sublimity of majestic nature. Far away to the left rolls a broad river, whose swift waters never upbore raft, or canoe, or bark of human construction; net, or spear, or barbed hook, never inflicted death upon one of the beautiful creatures that dwell in its deep recesses. The solemn forest extends to its very brink, but its proximity is betrayed by the wilder and more luxuriant vegetation to which it gives birth and sustenance. Myriads of wild flowers of every conceivable hue are gemming the earth; vines and creepers are twining like huge serpents around the trunks, and stretching their vast length from branch to branch of the gigantic trees; and from the virgin soil, enriched by the decaying vegetable deposits of ages, are springing thousands of shrubs, bushes, and mosses, that have never been classed by Linnæus.

But see! was ever prospect more glorious than the superb sweep of the eye from the descending slope, at the bottom of which rolls the mighty river? Fed by the streams of a thousand hills, its dark waters pour along, noiseless, gloomy, but swift, and second only in breadth to the giant Missouri. Who can tell from what distant and unvisited region has flowed the eternal stream that is hastening by, to mingle its waves with those of the trackless ocean? From what inaccessible snows trickle the numberless rills that unite in forming its source! What savage and unknown tribes are scattered over the wild luxuriant plains through which it sweeps in its lengthened career? The huge tree that is even now rushing by on its rapid resistless current, with its vast roots and wide-spreading branches towering over the flood, was perhaps torn from its native soil by an arctic tempest; the enormous trunk has perhaps voyaged thousands of miles since it was hurled from its abiding-place by the force of

the mighty wind, or still mightier waters on which it is now upborne, like a
feather dancing over the ripples of some diminutive fairy streamlet. Hark to the
loud splash of the leaping sturgeon ! Quick as the lightning's gleam, the strong
graceful creature darts from the river's bosom, scattering drops of brilliancy as
he springs, and instantly falling again with a sound that echoes along the shores,
while the circling waves spread, ring after ring, betraying the spot where he
fell. Far over the waters the opposite bank rises abruptly into a mountain
whose steep sides are covered with dark thick-growing evergreens ; the wild
laurel, and the juniper, and thousands of dwarfish cedars; but scattered about
are patches of cold dull gray, which tell of the naked rock, from whose bosom
the thin soil has been torn away by the rains and winds of past ages. And
see ! High over head soars a lordly eagle, gliding without an effort in wide
circles, far above the highest peak of the mountain, and covering space for an
empire with the keen glance of his strong vision. With a single sweep of his
mighty pinion he shoots away like an arrow from the bow of a vigorous moun-
taineer, and then with his wings wide-spread and motionless, he rushes through
the sustaining air, rejoicing in his unequalled speed, yet with a flight so calm
and true that not one plume of his arching neck is ruffled. Thousands of
yards beneath him, the broad stream lies, diminished in his gaze by distance
to a rivulet, glancing in the summer sun, and the huge rocks that topple on
the mountain's brow appear too small to give a resting-place for his expanded
talon ; yet not a living thing fit to become the prey of the noble bird can stir
upon the plain beyond, or in the shadow of those rocks, or by the waters of
the glittering stream, and pass unnoticed by the piercing eye that from its airy
height is glancing over the scene below. A wanton kid is playing in the joy
of its young heart among the cliffs, watched by the loving eyes of its wild dam,
that lies upon the breast of yonder naked rock, basking in the noontide beams.
The eagle's glance is for a moment fixed upon the thoughtless creature, glad in
the solitude that is its home ; but no feeling of compassion touches the heart
of the high-soaring bird ; he pauses for an instant in his circling flight—his
mighty wings are thrown above his head, and with a rush swift as the storm's,
but noiseless as the falling of the dew, he pounces on his victim ; a single
scream, wild as the whoop of the revenging savage, tells of his exultation, and
in another moment the fated kid is borne aloft, turning its dying eyes in vain
for help to its affrighted mother.

Turn from the feathered monarch of the air, and see another shape of beauty. The faint stealings of the breeze that now begins to murmur through the
foliage, are loaded with the fragrance of a thousand flowers ; and there, within
that level shade near which an enormous tulip-tree uprears its lofty trunk, is
the birthplace of the mingling odors. There grows the honeysuckle, twining
its prehensile stem around the branches of the sweet magnolia, and shedding
perfume with its myriad of flowers; there, too, grow the sweet-briar, and the
many-flowered rose ; the fragrant wild-apple and the beautiful catalpa. But
brilliant as they are, their splendor is eclipsed by the living form of perfect
loveliness, whose rapid movements baffle the eye, which vainly strives to follow

its almost viewless progress as it darts among the flowers like a winged gem, gathering from every one its sweets with but a single kiss. Rays of every hue and of the most perfect brilliance glitter from its plumage; and on its tiny head it wears a crest that gives out flashes like the diamond. The humming of its wings is scarcely louder than the drowsy note of the industrious bee with which it shares the nectar of the flowers. See! The splendid creature has darted like a sun-beam close to where I stand; I could reach it with the slender wand torn from the hazel-bush, beneath whose shade we saw the young oppossums gaily feeding. Shall I strike it to the earth? It is a bird; the least of the feathered race; the wonder and darling of the curious ornithologist. There! It has come still nearer, and I could grasp it with my hand—Perish the thought! How should I presume to ask or hope for mercy in my dying hour with the guilt upon my soul of having crushed that bright and beautiful existence? The God who made me, also made the humming-bird; endowed it with the capacity to feel, and suffer, and enjoy; and shall I dare to take the life to which its right is just as perfect as is mine to that which I possess, and for the sake too, of the very loveliness designed to give that life protection? Blighting and wasting in the act, the beauty which my cruel nature prompts me to pervert from the benevolent purpose of its Creator, and wrest into a motive of destruction? Go thy way unharmed, most innocent and lovely thing; the cruel hawk would spare a thing so exquisite, a life so made for joy and beauty; man alone would inflict suffering and death upon thee, and man is a stranger here.

There is a storm brewing among the hills. The faint breeze that was welcomed so lately, as it came stealing at intervals over the water whose bosom it scarce had power to ruffle, sweeps through the forest now, in short, fitful gusts, tossing the long slender branches in wild confusion, and whirling up the dead leaves from the earth upon which they are thickly strewed, yellow and withered, as if for an emblem of that certain doom to which all earthly things are subject.

In the pauses between, there is a fearful and ominous stillness, and the heat, which, intense as it was until now, has been tempered by the elastic freshness and purity of the atmosphere, is becoming close, heavy, and oppressive; thick black clouds are gathering over the mountain; and from the ancient trees issues a dismal and indescribable sound, that to the ear of fancy seems a groan of lamentation for the wrath of the expected tempest. It comes, at last, in its fury; the leaves are torn from their branches and scattered aloft by thousands upon the wings of the storm; sudden darkness, like that of midnight, broods over the earth; a few big drops of rain come plashing upon the thick masses of foliage, soon to be followed by a descending torrent; and the river's bosom, so calm and waveless but a few minutes since, is lashed into foam and ploughed up in huge heaving furrows by the rush of the hurricane. Hark to the roar of the thunder; the voice of Omnipotence calling the elements to battle. The lightning flashes, and all around is a blaze of fearful and unendurable splendor; millions of torches could not dispel the gloom of this old forest, overshadowed by the black storm-bearing clouds, with a more dazzling and intolerable radiance. Again and again it illuminates all the firmament; and see, how the forky streams play round the brow of the precipice! Heavens, what a terrific peal! Beginning with a sharp and sudden crack, succeeded by a continuous rattle, alike in sound, but louder than the volleyed ringing of ten thousand muskets, and ending with a roar, compared with which, the most appalling noises of human invention are but the distant murmur of a gentle stream, in contrast with the booming of an angry sea against the rocks of some bold cape or headland. Another peal, and yet more awful! Is it the day of doom? Down to your knees and pray, for surely the last trump is sounding to announce the awful moment in which earth shall pass away, and all that it contains be wrapt in one complete and terrible destruction. Impending ruin overhangs the bright and beautiful creation; but the Almighty hand controls the raging elements and his bidding has already gone forth to put a limit to their fury. The rain descends with tenfold violence; no longer in streams, but as it were in floods, that break not in their fall; yet is the howling of the wind less fierce and dreadful, and each succeeding thunder-peal is shorter and more distinct than the last. The intervals between the flashes of the lightning are longer in duration, and faint gleams of day are breaking through the gloom that overspreads the firmament. Hail to the first joyful sunbeam, piercing the riven clouds! And now how fast they roll away, and leave the brilliant blue of the clear skies unshrouded! The rain-drops pendant from the leaves, and from the tendrils of the vines, and resting in the bosom of the flowers, sparkle like countless diamonds in the sunlight; the air is cooled, and the hot earth refreshed, and the birds are again darting and pouring forth their melody among the foliage.

CHARLOTTE TEMPLE'S GRAVE.

A CORRESPONDENT of the Washington Chronicle, who recently visited Trinity churchyard, noting the quaint inscriptions on the stones and monuments, writes: "A particular slab which set me moralizing was one which probably not one of the countless throng that hurries past it down Broadway, is aware covers the remains of a once beautiful and fascinating woman, the record of whose romantic and sad career has touched the hearts of hundreds of thousands. The slab itself, the place where it lies, the strange excavation made in its upper part, and the simple name—'CHARLOTTE TEMPLE'—cut near the centre of the stone, is in itself material sufficient for a half dozen fictions such as are now-a-days manufactured 'on the shortest notice and most reasonable terms' for the sensation press. No date of birth, no indications of family, no date of death, appears on the slab; nothing but 'Charlotte Temple.' The legend runs that while only sixteen, she was courted by a dashing young British officer. He deserted her, and then—the old story—she died. A little daughter which she left, was tenderly cared for; at a proper age was taken to England, and a fortune of twenty thousand pounds settled upon her by the head of her father's family, the Earl of Derby. She, true daughter and true woman, came back to New York and erected this monument to the memory of her parent. The inscription upon it was engraved on a solid tablet of brass an inch in thickness, heavily plated with silver, and thus it read: ' Sacred to the memory of CHARLOTTE STANLEY, aged 19 years.' This filial duty performed, the daughter returned to England and lived a life of unobtrusive piety and usefulness until the history of her family was closed with the life of the late Earl. But the story of the plate or tablet is left to be told. Supposed to be of silver and of much value, it tempted the cupidity of those who feared not to desecrate the place of sepulture. On a dark night two men, with hammer and chisels, stealthily crept to its side, and succeeded in prying it from the slab; but, while making off, hearing, or fancying they heard, some one in pursuit, they dropped it in the grass, where it was subsequently found. They were never detected. The plate was not restored to its original place, and it was by some good heart, doubtless, who had known the deceased in her days of childhood, that the simple name, ' Charlotte Temple,' was afterward cut just underneath the excavation. There it may be seen, at any moment, within twenty feet of Broadway, by any one who will take the trouble to raise himself on the stones in which the iron fence is set, and glance toward the slab now almost imbedded in the turf."

LULU IS DEAD!

LIKE a fair, fragrant rose-bud when exposed to a chill night, she folded her sweetness within herself, and perished ere she had bloomed. No more shall we listen to her lisping prattle or watch her tiny steps. No more catch her in our arms, and kiss her warm rosy lips ! Like a shadow that has lingered with the sunshine, she has faded from view; her spirit has gone forth from earth, but her little body is yet here, though cold and still. There it reposes; not in her warm, comfortable little crib, but there in that little polished rosewood coffin, with bright silver nails and white satin lining. Her snow white frock, with its skirt folded in so many neat tucks, which she so loved to wear, her tight-fitting little stockings and her fairy-like shoes, are all on her now ; and her delicate waxen little hands, placed complacently over her breast, with fresh, fragrant and beautiful flowers, symbols of her pure little self, clasped between her tiny, taper fingers.

Death has not fixed his terribly rigid stamp upon those baby limbs and features. She lies there as though in a deep, sweet sleep ; the red blush of life has fled from her cheeks, but left the sea-shell's pale pink in its stead, and the azure of her dreamy eyes has only faded to a fainter blue, as seen through those closed transparent lids, the lashes of which lie calmly now over her marbled cheeks, and the hair seems as golden and glossy as in life, and those sweet bow lips retain the coral's tint and seem parted with a smile, but alas ! they can make no answer

now. She was—indeed—too bright, too pure, too beautiful a thing for earth ;
and so she has gone home to Heaven ! She came only to teach us how innocent and pure we too must become ere we can join the holy throng. She
came to teach that great lesson of our Saviour's to His disciples, when they went
unto him saying, " Who is the greatest in the kingdom of heaven ? " And he
called a little child to him and placed him in the midst of them, and said,
" Verily, I say unto you, except ye be converted and become as little children,
ye shall not enter into the kingdom of Heaven."

SUMMER IN MOUNT AUBURN.

Gone ! Dear reader, did you ever dwell upon the full significance of that one
little word—gone ? If you never have, say it to yourself when the sun has set
beyond the hills and left no reflection upon your hearthstone. Say it when you
wake from slumber and have dreamed out your dream and found it but a delu-
sion. And say it with us as this beautiful June morning we stroll through this
" city of the silent"—numbering the perished flowers and their brightness, whose
breath departed into Heaven. Is there not meaning in those four small charac-
ters ? Is there not cypress and yew clinging to their every curve ? Do they
not overhang the fountain of tears, and are they not lined with the color of the
heart ? And is there a fitter time or a more appropriate place to ponder this
moral, than whilst treading this " grave-land of the gone world ? "

The skies are cloudless, save where some white robed spirit-cloud swims amid
the etherial blue, floating like a departed soul far away to the golden gates of
Heaven. The wind, that solemn organist, allows his fingers to stray among the
strings of the Æolian harps that nature has hung in every tree-top, while according harmonies burst from every bird-throat, attuned in this solemn cathedral of
nature. " Passing away " swells on the breeze. " Passing away " echoes yon
waving cypress bough. " Sing away " rallies the winged wild bird. Grieved
into stillness by the mournful tone, while as we linger, our hearts in our ears,
and our eyes fixed on the earth-couch of beauty spread before us, through the
green aisles we hear the notes fading in the distance—" Away "—" Away," and
involuntarily we gaze upward and onward, as if following the spirit to its destiny
in Heaven. How many irresistible thoughts crowd upon us as we trace so many
voiceless witnesses of the last great change. By how many a hearthstone has
the light gone out and its sacred ashes entombed here. Children and young
men and maidens ; aged men and women, weeds swaying in the wind of years ;
manhood, with bold brow and strong arm and stout heart ; maternity, with its
tenderness and infancy in its purity and beauty.

Here, upon a pure white slab, traced by the sculptor's hand, we read : " Our
Fanny." This and a rosebud folded—nothing more. Upon the leaf of time had
only been written the name of the fair young creature, and then amid birds
and flowers—

They laid her 'neath the bending billow,
    Beneath the summer sun;
Bright curls resting on the snowy pillow
    Of the angelic one.

And the measure of the story must be filled in Heaven. The rose and the violet may blend their lines above her, but the living flower is far away adorning the fields of light. The glad spring birds may carol here and call forth the glad playmates in the olden home; but the silent songster is tuning her golden harp before the " Shepherd who gathers the lambs in his bosom."

Here, in proud bronze, with colossal head and the elements of mightiness and insignia of great attainments, is built the monument of the benefactor of science —now called to cross that dark, mysterious tide with Death's ferryman alone. Science followed him through life, but it could not guide his bark or fill his sail when the boat put forth into the Unknown. There, with 'remembrances and memorials which stretch far back to the birth of time and the creation of man, and with marbled " memento mori " modelled even from the greatness of Scipio, lays—

    " A head upon its lap of earth
    And sweetly mouldering into it,"

which in life brought forth the hidden mysteries of the mind and established them within the curving brow and swelling temples. Alas! the earth-worm erects its palace within that cunning brain, and the clod presses the throbbing temples instead of the soft hand and the kiss of love. Here, within this miniature palace holds wealth, the last, sad drapery it can ever hold, or canopy above its foster-child. The silken couch was exchanged for the narrow tomb, and the costly robe for the straightened shroud. There is one great event for all, and the messenger of Death is regardless whether his portal be a gate of thorns, or across a marble threshold.

" Our Father," breathes a silent slab, which tells to the heart how the pride and the mainstay of some household band was called to the dim land, away from the group who put forth their hands to save him.

And the withered rose on the adjacent column appeals for the delicate bride who vanished like a rainbow in midsummer, relinquishing her life ere she had reached its June, fading from her husband's arms into the silent grave. The inverted torch, the broken column, the blasted wheat-spear have each a story and a poem within them, and crave alike a tear.

Mount Auburn—how beautiful the name—with beautiful suggestions —

    " Leading the traveller from the Vale of Tears,
    When life's great work is done,
    Through Time's great labyrinth of years
    To a calm, sweet Auburn of its own."

But we turn away, thinking how the birds will build in these branches, summer after summer, and sing their requiems, until in their turn they pass into the

Paradise of Birds. How the dews, those tears the stars have wept, will mingle with the tears of earth's children, and keep the sod green above these quiet sleepers when we, too, have lain down in some quiet spot to be forgotten.

We pass through the granite portal, and once more looking back through this beautiful treasure-house, cannot but catch the sighings of the breeze as it sweeps onward, murmuring —

That Heaven is nearer than mortals think
    When they look with a trembling dread
At the misty future that stretches on
    From the silent home of the dead;
That when the silver cord is loosed—
    When the veil is rent away,
Solemn and sweet will the passage be
    To the flower-land far away.

LITTLE CHARLIE — A LAMENT.

BY T. B. ALDRICH.

O, Sunshine, making golden spots .
    Upon the carpet at my feet—
The shadows of the coming flowers!
The phantoms of forget-me-nots
    And roses red and sweet!—
How can you seem so full of joy,
    And we so sad at heart and sore ?—
Angel of death! again thy wings
    Are folded at our door!

We can but yearn through length of days
For something lost we fancied ours;
We'll miss thee, darling, when the Spring
    Has touched the world to flowers!
For thou wast like that dainty month
Which strews the violet at its feet:
Thy life was slips of golden sun
And silver tear-drops braided sweet!
For thou wast light and thou wast shade,
And thine were sweet capricious ways!—
Now lost in purple languors, now
No bird in ripe-red summer days
    Was half as wild as thou!

O little presence! everywhere
We find some touching trace of thee—

A pencil mark upon the wall
That " naughty hands " made thoughtlessly ;
And broken toys around the house—
Where he has left them they have lain,
Waiting for little busy hands
   That will not come again,—
   Will never come again !

Within the shrouded room below
He lies a-cold—and yet we know
   It is *not* Charlie there !
It is not Charlie cold and white,
It is the robe, that, in his flight,
   He gently cast aside !
Our darling hath not died !

O rare pale lips ! O clouded eyes !
   O violet eyes grown dim !
Ah, well ! this little lock of hair
   Is all of him !
Is all of him that we can keep
For loving kisses, and the thought
Of him and death may teach us more
Than all our life hath taught !

God, walking over starry spheres,
   Did clasp his tiny hand,
And led him, through a fall of tears,
   Into the Mystic Land !

Angel of death ! we question not :
Who asks of heaven, " Why does it rain ? "
Angel ! we bless thee, for thy kiss
   Hath hushed the lips of Pain !
No " Wherefore ? " or " To what good end ? "
Shall out of doubt and anguish creep
Into our thought. We bow our heads :
   He giveth His beloved sleep !

LIFE.—A spirit on high flings us into this life, and then counts thirty, forty, seventy, or eighty, as we do when we roll a stone down an abyss, and by the time he has counted thus far, he hears our final, sullen plunge into the grave.

BOOKS.—Books are leaves, thrown, to sink or swim, into the stream of time, by a being who soon plunges in after them.

SUMMER LIFE IN NEW-ENGLAND.

BY HARRIET MARTINEAU.

IF I lived in Massachusetts, my residence during the hot months should be beside one of its ponds. These ponds are a peculiarity in New-England scenery very striking to the traveller. Geologists tell of the time when the valleys were chains of lakes; and in many places the eye of the observer would detect this without the aid of science. There are many fields and clusters of fields of remarkable fertility, lying in basins, the sides of which have much the appearance of the greener and smoother dikes of Holland. These suggest the idea of their having been ponds at the first glance. Many remain filled with clear water, the prettiest meres in the world. A cottage on Jamaica Pond, for instance, within an easy ride of Boston, is a luxurious summer abode. I know of one unequalled in its attractions, with its flower garden, its lawn, with its banks, shelving down to the mere; banks dark with rustling pines, from under whose shade the bright track of the moon may be seen, lying cool on the rippling waters. A boat is moored in the cove at hand. The cottage itself is built for coolness, and its broad piazza is draperied with vines, which keep out the sun from the shaded parlors.

The way to make the most of a summer's day in a place like this is to rise at four, mount your horse, ride through the lanes for two hours, finding breakfast ready on your return. If you do not ride, you slip down to the bathing-house on the creek; and, once having closed the door, have the shallow water completely at yourself, carefully avoid going beyond the deep water-mark, where no one knows how deep the mere may be. After breakfast you should dress your flowers, before those you gather have quite lost the morning dew. The business of the day, be it what it may, housekeeping, study, teaching, authorship, or charity, will occupy you till dinner at two. You have your dessert called into the piazza, where, catching glimpses of the mere through the wood on the banks, your water-melon tastes cooler than within, and you have a better chance of a visit from a pair of humming birds. You retire to your room, all shaded with green blinds, lie down with a book in your hand, and sleep soundly for two hours at least. When you wake and look out, the shadows are lengthening on the lawn, and the hot haze has melted away. You hear a carriage behind the fence, and conclude that friends from the city are coming to spend the evening with you. They sit within till after tea, telling you that you are living in the sweetest place in the world. When the sun sets you all walk out, dispersing in the shrubbery, or on the banks. When the moon shows herself above the opposite woods, the merry voices of the young people are heard from the cove, where the boys are getting out the boat. You stand, with a companion or two, under the pines, watching the progress of the skiff, and the receding splash of the oars. If you had any one as I had to sing German popular songs to you, the enchantment is all the greater. You are capriciously lighted home by fireflies, and there is your table covered with fruit and iced lemonade. When your friends have left you, you would fain forget it is time to rest ; and your last act before you sleep is to look out once more from your balcony upon the silent mere and moonlit lawn.

POETRY.

THE poetry of imagination, although it may glitter more, is neither so rich nor so glorious as the poetry of the heart. We have very few poets of the latter description. In childhood, and sometimes in youth, we are alive to the poetry of the heart. While the mind is pure and artless, devoid of any thing that can be termed sinful—free from anxious and corroding cares, all nature appears to us very much as Eden appeared to our first parents. Every thing upon which we gaze seems to be good, and lovely, and beautiful. Our hearts claim acquaintance with all that meets the eye, and we feel deeply impressed by every little event which takes place around us. To such poetry as this, the beautiful inhabitants of another world are no doubt awake ; and as they touch their golden harps, their living souls seem to leap among the strings, and float on the harmonious notes, as they arise like incense to the great Fountain of love and joy. In this world poetry does not always mingle with devotion, though I believe that a poetic soul is generally impressed more earnestly with devout sentiments than those minds which are of a more earthly cast. But I believe in the world to come, poetry and devotion become melted into one— that we are rendered keenly and acutely sensitive to all with which we hold intercourse, and thus our bliss comes heightened into continual rapture. Indeed, the representations of Heaven which we have in the Scriptures, appear to favor such an opinion.

SELF-EXAMINATION.—Few sufficiently practice the habit of self-examination. Through life man is liable to error, and requires check, rebuke and council. He should personify his own conscience. He should be his own good spirit, hovering over himself in moments of passion, temptation and danger, and reminding himself that he owes a duty to his Maker, with which the opinions and consequences of the world have nothing to do. Life, in regard to the world, is a passing dream. The reality is the *hereafter*. Moral principle is cherished and strengthened by self-examination, which continually instructs him in broad and magnanimous duties. In the calmness of solitude, passion and error relax their hold, and the mists of the world disperse. Truth dwells there, and, with her holy voice, reviews, sanctions, or condemns the past, and directs the future. Habituate yourself to take indulgent and exculpatory views of those with whom you live, with such exceptions as moral courage and firmness require, and as you can render good reasons for.

Editor's Table.

Thoughts for the Season.

AGAIN the queen of the summer months is with us, and her usual pleasant accompaniments are not wanting. She was as welcome last year, as the year before, and in '61 we are as eager as ever to grasp the treasures of the sixth month, although her advent is no new thing. Though it is annually marked by the same characteristics, how fresh and beautiful all of June's gifts seem at this, the present time; her flowers and foliage, and the healthful breezes which toss upward and backward the green leaves, and gently sway the branches of many a noble tree, her changes from cloud to sunlight, and the vivid contrast of verdure and heavenly blue, are all parts of one grand whole, which could never constitute a monotony of sight and sound.

We have said that June is welcome as ever, but we did not add that there is a difference in her coming which awakens in many an admiration more appreciative than before of the bright mantle of beauty which has been thrown upon all things. She comes now in the midst of strife where before was peace, and although she finds the hearts of all stirred with patriotic feeling, how many does she not find anxious for the friends who have nobly gone forth to take their part in a struggle which is as likely to cause the loss of one as another. Husbands may leave wife and family, sons bid farewell to parents and kindred, animated by the one desire to espouse the cause of right, and faithfully fight under the banner which is dear to them; Spartan mothers may bid their sons go with their blessing, and return only when victory is announced, but under all this disguise there is hidden now, in excitement, feelings which quiet surely brings forth. Not a doubt enters the mind that duty now calls soldiers to the field, and that military action is unavoidable; but the question is, whether future victory, glorious victory, can heal the wounded hearts already stricken, letting alone all thought and calculation of the numbers, few or many, whose destiny on earth may end as suddenly as the first fallen.

Does not June unfold her buds, send forth her singing birds, perfume the balmy air with fragrance all in vain for the parents, whose pride of life, the staff and stay of their old age, the noble, brave, rash ELLSWORTH, to whom but a short time ago a good-bye was bidden by him, as he tarried at the threshold, with words of comfort and promise; are the glories of the early summer productive of any but agonizing recollections in one gentle heart whose farewell was lingering and but half spoken; whose light of life, with all the rainbow promises of the future has been withdrawn, and only the consolation left that he died, a brave but imprudent soldier?

Can the young wife of LIEUTENANT GREBBLE, of glorious memory, reconcile herself to the idea that there is to be no coming home, no warm clasp of hands, and warmer welcoming, nothing but a placing away in silence a cold form, which is but an image of the gallant soldier who stood by his cannon to the last, and whose conduct will afford a bright example for time to come; can the bride of less than a year part without a murmur from one whose life was part and parcel of hers?

N. P. Willis, from whose pen are now emanating "Lookings on at the War," relates an incident which fully illustrates the heartlessness of some, and we trust they are few, whose feelings, by luxury and fashion, are deadened to every thing which does not immediately concern themselves or friends. It also comes in as a thought congenial with our own, at the present moment. The incident he thus describes: " At Havre de Grace the long covered passage by which we passed from the ferry to the cars, was occupied as a temporary barrack for one of the regiments. The soldiers in their blue uniforms and Kossuth hats were, off duty, of course, sitting in groups or lying asleep on the floor, with knapsacks for pillows, their arms stacked at short distances; and the pathway in the centre, by which the hundred or two railway passengers made their way, with the more accustomed belongings of travel—cloaks and carpet-bags, umbrellas and bundles, tired women and crying children—was so narrow as to bring into curiously striking contrast the doings of peace and war. A showy and handsome school-girl, who had sat behind me in the cars, all excitement and high spirits with the prospect of a vacation that was to be enlivened with the soldiering in her neighborhood, caught her flounces as she swept dancingly along, upon the chafed and bare feet of a sleeping recruit. Helping to disengage her, I took a second look at the poor fellow, who lay undisturbed on his back. He had taken off his shoes to drop asleep, very tired, upon the bare floor; but his chance attitude with his arm under his head, and the remarkable beauty of the boy (for he looked scarce seventeen, and the down of a raven mustache just darkened the corners of his well-cut lip) made a picture that an artist would have remembered. He looked like the lad who, at home, was his mother's idol, and who had left tears and prayers behind to follow him to the wars, perhaps to be shot and mourned over, perhaps to be a hero of history—and there, as he rested from his hard service, this thoughtless beauty swept her costly silk over his bleeding feet, and though tangled to him as she passed, never stopping her gay prattle, nor giving him a look! And thus closely and unconsciously come together, sometimes, the comedy and tragedy of this varied life!"

Orphan and Destitute Children.

THERE are some whose work in this world is so unpretending and quiet that the credit which ought to be freely bestowed for their actions, is lost to sight for want of the setting-forth which noisier actors on the world's stage procure for their own deeds. There is no cause of more importance than that of orphan and destitute children, nor one which can be better productive of greater heart pleasure in the end to the benefactor of such, and as the satisfaction of nobly doing one's duty is all the reward to be obtained, it is very evident that those engaging in it must be influenced by the highest and holiest motives. The following modest report of a score of years' service in the work of love and charity, is submitted by Mr. Joseph M. Hale, of Boston, one of the most earnest philanthropists in the vicinity.

" Twenty years have passed since I enlisted in the cause of procuring homes for Orphan and Destitute Children, and I look back upon my labors in the proud satisfaction that they have not been in vain. During this term of service, I have obtained homes for *one hundred and fifteen* little ones, who are yet happy and contented. Nor have I lost sight of any of them, for a large number of them I have visited, and with the others I have maintained a continuous correspondence. I have still in my possession a large number of letters, which are deeply interesting to me. It is gratifying to look around me and see some of these children holding positions of trust, who, had they been left uncared for might have been pests to society, and a disgrace to the nation.

One boy, a man now, is foreman of a large machine shop; another a meritorious fancy painter. One is engaged in the express business; another is a student in the legal profession. Three have come into possession of considerable property.

These gratifying results are incitements to continued labor, and while I would not complain, it is but justice to myself to say, that I am the agent of no society or association, but depend upon the voluntary contributions of my friends, and the friends of the cause. Notwithstanding I have often been pinched in my business, still a way has been opened for me, and thus far, my labors have been successful.

My enlistment is for life, and I dare not go back. I have been so long familiar to the public, and am able to turn to such undoubted references, in all professions and callings in society, that I am persuaded that the cause and the labor both enjoy the confidence of the public.

With heart-felt thanks for what the friends of the cause have done, I have only to present its claims before you, humbly hoping for a continuance of your kindly consideration and assistance.

JOSEPH M. HALE."

The Tour.

UPPER ELM AVENUE.

THE first lot on the left side of Upper Elm Avenue is the large inclosure of Peter Hubbell, which is surrounded by a massive iron fence, set in a handsome curbing of Quincy granite; it is approached by steps of the same material. In the further corner, at the right, is a monument of marble in the shape of a cross, upon the horizontal bar of which is inscribed I. H. S., the initials of the Latin designation of the Saviour. Below, upon the die, is the inscription in memory of " Fannie C. Swope, wife of Rev. C. E. Swope, and daughter of the late Rev. J. Prentiss, of Catskill, N. Y., died September 1, 1856, aged 29 years." Below are added the words:

" Blessed are the pure in heart."

Adjoining this is the Knight monument, a cut of which, together with an inscription, we published on Page 11, Vol. II. Upon the south side of the larger structure we find an inscription stating it to be " A tribute of affection to Elizabeth S. Knight, 1852." Near the gate, the smaller marble memorial bears upon its front the inscription: " One Lord, One Faith, One Baptism." Upon the scroll on the west side is perpetuated the memory of " Elizabeth S. Knight, born in West Framingham, May 23, 1794, died in Boston, September 10, 1852, in hope of eternal life." Upon another side are the Scriptural extracts:

" God is love. Thy loving kindness is better than life; in Thy presence is fullness of joy. At Thy right hand there are pleasures evermore."

The Atherton lot, No. 1725, has a good supply of foliage, as a front adornment, in the shape of two spreading maples. The monument is situated in the middle of the inclosure; it is of marble, elaborately worked. Above the die rises a panelled column, surmounted by a heavy cap hung with wreaths. Upon the east side of the die is an inscription to the memory of " Susan Baker, wife of Samuel Atherton, died May 18, 1858, aged 25 years." On the opposite side we find inscribed the name of " Temple Holbrook, wife of Samuel Atherton, died February 24, 1849, aged 80 years; Thomas H., son of Samuel and T. H. Atherton, died May 14, 1845, aged 2 years and 9 months." Adjoining this is No. 1853, owned by Isaac Stickney; it is uninclosed, but has shrubbery in front. We come next to No. 2055, of which Charles W. Pierce is the proprietor. Here we find a small headstone to " Emily Frances, died June 10, 1852, aged 17 months." Near this is a larger memorial to " Rev. Jotham Horton, died in Boston, February 28, 1853, aged 54 years. A faithful minister of Jesus Christ, and fearless advocate of the cause of the lowly and oppressed." Another, to the right of the latter, bears the name of " Mrs. Judith, wife of Rev. Jotham Horton, died October 28, 1847, aged 48 years." This sentence is added: " I die in the faith of our Lord, Jesus Christ, a sinner saved by grace, in full and blessed hope of a glorious immortality."

Random Sketches.

Lots of R. Ridlan and Lydia S. Gale.

On the north side of Indian Ridge, at the point where the ridge path joins Central Avenue, improvements have lately been made by constructing terraces, which form a part of Numbers 2931 and 345; of these Richard Ridlan and Lydia S. Gale are the respective owners. On the terraced side, about the lowest portion, there are flower beds edged with granite; a little higher up, a gravel walk leads to granite steps, which in turn lead up to Indian Ridge Path. Both lots are handsomely curbed, the terraces affording a good opportunity for the display of such a method of inclosure.

The new monument on the first consists of a granite plinth, marble base, die, second base, and column, the last being surmounted by a garlanded urn. On the south side we find an inscription to the memory of " Emmeline and her children." Below are the lines:

"As bowed by sudden storms the rose
Sinks on the garden's breast,
Down to the grave our sister goes,
In silence there to rest."

The second monument consists of granite plinth, marble base, and scroll-formed die; above the last is a second base, surmounted by a column, and an urn above an elaborate projection completes the structure. On the south side we find inscribed the names of " William A. Gale, died April 15, 1847, aged 51 years; Maria M. Gale, his wife, died April 18, 1828, aged 21." On the west side is an inscription perpetuating the memory of " Elizabeth Gale, died September 13, 1847, aged 77 years; Elizabeth Gale, died September 16, 1856, aged 68 years." On the north side there is another to " William Gale, died June 20, 1812, aged 66 years; Hannah P. Gale, his wife, died March 2, 1830, aged 72 years."

Lucy Dudley Hall.

The Lot in which Lucy Dudley Hall is interred, is No. 2889 Oak Avenue. A beautiful white marble monument, in the north-east corner, has a rose carved upon it, and bears the name of LUCY.

SWEET LUCY.

In memory of LUCY DUDLEY HALL, who died May 8, 1859.

Should it be cause for deep distress,
For tears, and sobs, and anguish sore,
That earth has one sweet child the less,
And Heaven has one bright angel more?

Life,—long or short,—is little worth;
What recks it in reality—
Be life but long enough on earth
To win Heaven's immortality?

Life's holiest, freshest, morning hours,
To this sweet opening bud were given—
Which closed its dewy eyes on earth,
To open them in Heaven!

Say not—" she died;" it were more just
To say, she then was born;
The Night which gathered dark round us
For her was glorious Morn!

Through the " dark valley " where dismayed,
Earth's mightiest cry—" Thy staff! Thy
rod ! "
Unconscious of its gloomy shade—
Fearless the little pilgrim trod!

Too slowly in our Northern clime,
Blossom'd for her the tardy spring;
She has reached a world of sunshine,—
Where no sweet bud lies withering.

Sweet Lucy ! in that glance of thine,—
Those holy, sweet, seraphic eyes,—
We might have read the warning sign,
Which marked thee early for the skies.

Endow'd with every winning grace,
A spirit loving, bright, and clear,—
We might have known that angel face
Had wandered from some holier sphere.

If, in the glorious new birth
A new celestial grace is given,—
She was so cherub-like on earth,
What must she be in Heaven!

Fling around this gather'd Lily,
Spring's first sweet buds and blossoms fair;
Round this brow so marble chilly,
Smooth the soft rings of auburn hair.

Lay the small white hands together,
Close the pure, sweet, dove-like eyes.
Ah, these earthly blossoms wither—
She shall bloom beyond the skies !

Weep not! she had the best of earth,—
Its radiant, sunlit, dewy morn;
She pluck'd life's fairest, freshest flowers,
Nor lived to know they bore a thorn !

Weep not ! for she has done with tears !
She early called to realms of bliss!
What weary patriarch's lengthen'd years
Can reach a close more blest than this?

But the young parents, who to rest,
In quiet Auburn's flowery sod,
Bear weeping back their bright, their blest,
And leave her in the arms of God !

May faith, supported by " the Rock,"
See, though quick tears their vision dim
The fairest lambs of all the flock,
Are fittest offerings for Him.

And may they prove, in trusting faith,
That as they would have striven
To lead her infant steps on earth,—
She shall lead theirs to Heaven.

IN 1831, Mount Auburn, the first rural cemetery in the United States, was consecrated; since that time there has been a great change in the places of burial, till now nearly every city has its beautiful resting-place for the dead, in its environs.

Record of Interments at Mount Auburn Cemetery.

Numb.	Date (1861).	Name of Deceased.	Where from.	Age. y. m. d.	Date of Death.	No. of Lot.
10,335	May 2	Child of J. Duncan	Boston	8 27	April 30, 1861	816
10,336	3	Sarah Bagnall	Chelsea	82	May 1,	504
10,337	3	Emily P. Moore	Cambridge	3 9 26	3,	2443
10,338	4	Abner Ellis	Boston	72 5 3	Aug. 24, 1859	3098
10,339	6	Myra Neal Morse	Cambridge	5 8 28	May 4, 1801	1788
10,340	7	Anna P. Barnard	Charlestown	38 4 10	5,	R. T.
10,341	7	Caroline Amling	Chelsea	50	4,	1770
10,342	8	Maria J. Bagley	Boston	9	Feb. 20, 1837	1539
10,343	8	Edward W. Bagley	Boston	9 5	April 13, 1847	1539
10,344	8	Samuel C. Thacher	Boston	44 9	May 6, 1861	936
10,345	8	William B. Hill	Boston	18 4 10	6,	R. T.
10,346	11	Samuel N. Spooner	Boston	12 11 10	11,	3087
10,347	12	Sarah E. Amory	Boston	10 3 7	10,	2006
10,348	14	Abigail Kent	Boston	58 4	11,	2412
10,349	15	Child of A. Chamberl'n	Boston		14,	1245
10,350	15	Chastina Cullis	Boston	25 1	13,	
10,351	15	Frances A. Sortwell	Somerville	6 2 11	Aug. 19, 1857	3094
10,352	16	Child of R. T. Sprague	Boston		May 16, 1861	1274
10,353	16	Julia A Warriner	Boston	45 5 5	14,	409
10,354	17	Lucy D. Shattuck	Boston	57 6 12	15,	575
10,355	17	Charles S. Wiggin	Boston	19 24	14,	923
10,356	18	Thomas Child	Brighton	82 4	8,	
10,357	19	Fannie M. Farrington	Waltham	1 1 3	17,	467 S. J's
10,358	20	Wentworth Arris	Boston	43	Feb. 7,	778
10,359	20	Anna Cora Baker	Boston	8	May 19,	468 S. J's
10,360	20	A. M. Aspinwall	Boston	69 9	18,	2491
10,361	22	E. G. Howe	Boston	54 11	19,	2651
10,362	23	John E. Fader	Boston	9	Nov. 28, 1844	3072
10,363	24	Martha M. Cox	Boston	20 5 16	March 24, 1861	2328
10,364	25	Child of W. S. Leland	Reading		May 24,	1880
10,365	26	Anna R Bigelow	Cambridge	44 6 21	24,	
10,366	28	Hannah P. Pratt	Melrose			3112
10,367	28	Catherine Padelford	Boston	32	27,	470 S J's
10,368	28	George W. Vaughan	Boston	30	26,	R. T.
10,369	29	Eliza J. Gilman	Boston	37	27,	471 S. J's
10,370	29	William D. Bacon	New York,	6	April 25, 1860	3092
10,371	29	Charlotte E. Chapman	Longmeadow	5 11 23	Feb. 1, 1858	1158
10,372	29	Priscilla Kilhan	Boston	82	May 27, 1861	
10,373	30	Jenny E. Bowen,	Bedford	6 4 8		3114
10,374	30	Nathaniel W. Emery	Charlestown	21 11	Dec. 10, 1859	3117
10,375	30	Lemuel Shaw	Boston	80 2 21	March 30, 1861	
10,376	30	Ruth Green	Waltham	38 3 12	May 27,	1243
10,377	31	Hosea Ballou, 2d.	Somerville	64 7 9	27,	2942
10,378	31	Mary A. Stone	Cambridge	44	29,	2443
10,379	31	Frank P. Hathaway	Boston	6 16	Jan. 26,	3102
10,380	31	Currie Louise Slater	Boston	8 7	March 21,	2434
10,381	June 1	Mary E. Whitcomb	Malden	1 4	Nov. 15, 1858	3116
10,382	1	Mary H. Whitcomb	Malden	25 8 26	March 29, 1861	3116
10,383	2	Ann Simmons	Boston	63	May 30,	585
10,384	4	F. W. A. Smith	Boston	30 10	June 2,	473
10,385	5	Hannah E. Taylor	Newburyport	26	4,	216
10,386	5	Clara E. Stetson	Boston	32 3 10	2,	2128
10,387	5	William Tufts	Salem	74	3,	849
10,388	6	Robert Bacon	Winchester	83 3	4,	160
10,389	6	Harriet N. Dustin	Cambridge	10 8 9	5,	539
10,390	7	Mary C. Brown	Boston	2 2	5,	104
10,391	10	Susan Dwight	East Boston	81 0 11	8,	535
10,392	11	Mehitable Davis	Cambridge	68 2 8	8,	2503
10,393	11	Amasa C. Park	W. Newton		Sept. 12, 1813	1402
10,394	11	Eveline Stone	Belmont	61	June 9, 1861	
10,395	12	George Lombard	Boston	42 4 7	9,	150
10,396	13	James D Russell	Brighton	61	10,	100
10,397	13	Eliza M. Stevens	New York	33 3 29	6,	474 S. J's
10,398	13	Charles Lane	Boston		11,	2006
10,399	18	John F. Campbell	East Boston	4 3 17	16,	3024
10,400	18	Mary C. Lawrence	Boston	16 8 10	16,	2614
10,401	18	Rebecca P. Jarvis	Cambridge	80 6	15,	1072
10,402	20	George T. Carruth	Chelsea	42	April 21	
10,403	20	Almerin Bemis	Charlestown	36 5	June 19,	

Ornamental Iron Works.

The facilities for procuring Ornamental Iron Work of all kinds, either for House, Garden, or Cemetery purposes, are constantly increasing, so that it is now no longer necessary to run from one blacksmith shop to another in search of any desirable pattern. Those in want have only to call on Messrs. HENDERSON & Co., (who are general agents), to obtain any thing in the line that is wanted, *at the lowest rates.* They have the advantage of a beautiful room, well located, and have had much experience in the business. Their display of Garden Figures from their balcony fronting School Street, is daily witnessed by thousands, and their success with all their advantages of attracting and retaining customers is sure.

IRON FENCES.

IN this department, we find Messrs. "HENDERSON & Co." up with the times. They have a fine display of Samples at their salesroom, and their prices are so low that no one can find fault; another grand feature in their management is that of promptness; the lack of which which has been the ruin of many houses, otherwise deserving, perhaps. These gentlemen never keep a customer waiting unnecessarily, *one day* after the time set, for the execution of a contract.

Particular attention is paid not only in the *putting together*, but in the *putting up* of their Fences, so that when up, there is no *shake* to them, as is sometimes observed, where work has been carelessly done. Also in the *painting*, they put on a heavy undercoating to prevent the Iron from rusting. This, though of a little additional expense to the builder, *pays in the long run.*

IRON BEDSTEADS.

The value of these Bedsteads has been well tested in Boston and vicinity, and their use in the warm months, is almost a necessity. Vermin will, in spite of every effort which a careful housekeeper may put forth, locate themselves in *Wooden Bedsteads*, and spread all over the house; but by the use of these *Iron Bedsteads*, protection is *almost always sure.*

HENDERSON & CO.,
134 Washington Street, . . . BOSTON.
OVER MUNROE'S BOOKSTORE.

Funeral Wreaths and Flowers

PRESERVED,

TASTEFULLY ARRANGED AND NEATLY FRAMED,

AT SHORT NOTICE.

These Flowers are not *pressed*, but so *preserved*, as to retain

THEIR NATURAL FORM AND COLOR,

The public are respectfully invited to call and examine specimens at

MASSACHUSETTS

HORTICULTURAL SEED STORE.

A. C. BOWDITCH,

74 Tremont Street,

Opposite the Tremont House, ... BOSTON,

Or corner of Magazine and Perry Streets, Cambridgeport.

Wreaths and Memorial Flowers.

We adorn the nuptial altar with wreaths, and strew flowers over the biers of our dead. Many have desired to preserve these floral memorials of joy and sorrow. That desire can now be fulfilled. Flowers are preserved in all their perfection of form and color by a process which AZELL C. BOWDITCH, of the Horticultural Seed Store, No. 74 Tremont Street, opposite the Tremont House, has successfully adopted. Thus flowers that have decked the bridal bower, or have been laid upon the coffins of departed friends, may be preserved in unfading freshness. Mr. BOWDITCH gives his particular attention to this new and interesting branch of floral art. The specimens which may be examined in his store will well repay one for a visit.—*Daily Atlas & Bee.*

WAR IS THE CAUSE
— OF THESE —
DESTRUCTIVE PRICES.

All Who are in want of Dry Goods,
READ THIS:

1263 yards of Spring Silks, from 25 to 50 cents.
1991 do   do   do   from 50 to 75 cents.
2109 do   Silks, very superior, from 75 cents to $1.50.
640 do   Super do   do   do $1.50 to $3.25.
100 Crape Shawls will be sold from $2.50 to $50.00.
300 Stella Shawls, at any price.
756 Cashmere Long and Square Shawls, from $3.00 to $40.00.
Woolen Shawls in piles.
Capes and Spring Garments in great variety.

ALL WILL BE SOLD TO CLOSE THE STOCK.

300 Cashmere Scarfs, from 12½ cents to $7.50.
50,000 pairs of French Kid Gloves, 25 to 62 cents.

AN IMMENSE QUANTITY OF

HOSIERY, LISLE THREAD, AND SILK GOODS.

☞ REMEMBER, that this is a BANKRUPT STOCK of one of the

Largest Importers in New York,

AND MUST BE SOLD!

15 Cases of FINE PRINTS, 6¼ cents.
15 Cases of BEST MADDER, 9 cents.

☞ Here is one of the BEST STOCKS of

DRESS GOODS IN BOSTON!
☞ READ ON! ☜

19,000 yards of DE LAINES and CASHMERES, 8 to 12½ cents.
23 cases of SUPERIOR GREY GOODS, from 12½ cents to the best in the market.

White Goods,
Linens,
Domestics,
Parasols,

ALL AT A GREAT DISCOUNT!

Any Lady or Gentleman that has got to buy $25.00 worth of

DRY GOODS, THIS SPRING,

If they live within 150 miles of Boston, will SAVE MONEY by selecting from this
IMMENSE STOCK.

Let EVERYBODY come, and bring their friends with them.

☞ This sale will close the business, and the Store will be let.

No. 66 Hanover Street, ... BOSTON,
UNDER THE AMERICAN HOUSE.

A. J. GRIFFIN.

REMOVAL.

E. A. TEULON,

CARD ENGRAVER,

HAS TAKEN THE STORE

No. 284 Washington Street,

(Lately occupied by Mr. H. F. ZAHM,)

THREE DOORS NORTH OF BEDFORD STREET,

WHERE CAN BE FOUND

Every Description of Fine Card Engraving,

— SUCH AS —

INVITATION CARDS, "RECEPTION," "AT HOME," AND "CHURCH BIL-
LETS," FOR WEDDINGS,

Together with various kinds and styles of Cards for Visiting Purposes, all of which shall
be engraved in the most fashionable styles, and at reasonable prices.

CONSTANTLY ON HAND

A Choice Variety of Wedding Envelopes, Cake Boxes, &c.

ALSO,

Mourning Cards, Note Paper, Envelopes, &c.

BOSTON, JAN. 5th, 1859.

MESSRS. WILLIAMS & EVERETT having sold my entire stock of Cards, Envelopes and
Wedding Stationery, to MR. E. A. TEULON, I respectfully solicit for him the continuance of the
patronage hitherto extended to myself in that department, by my former patrons and friends.

All Card Plates left with me by my customers, can be found at Mr. Teulon's Office.

N. D. COTTON.

E. A. TEULON,

CARD ENGRAVER,

No. 284 Washington Street, Boston.

THREE DOORS NORTH OF BEDFORD STREET.